"Time is an illusion."
Albert Einstein.
"There is something going on in time, and space,
and beyond time and space, which, whether we like
it or not, spells duty."
Winston Churchill

Under A Blitz Sky

A NOVELLA BY
Kelly Ann Hambly

Dedicated to Paige and Danny

Chapter One

I'm standing in the small back bedroom of our cottage. The ceiling is low and slanted, with dark beams full of cobwebs, and the walls are peeling with layers upon layers of paint, as though they were unravelling pages upon pages of stories. If these walls could talk, I'm sure they wouldn't have anything nice to say. Why? Because this cottage was once owned by my great-great-grandfather, Seamus Jones. According to the family, he was somewhat of a local legend during the Second World War. However, the story has remained a family secret ever since, and I don't think my mum knows the entire story or she would've told me. Mum says the story has been altered so much, with little details added and taken away to the point where nobody knows the truth anymore or even if he existed. Which I think is a bit far-fetched, as he owned this house, and well, I wouldn't be here now if he hadn't.

The cottage is so old, creaky, and dusty that it gives me the creeps, especially this room overlooking fields and a derelict farmhouse just beyond the hedge separating our gardens.

The lightbulb swings from the ceiling above my head, catching me on the temple, and the incessant ticking of clocks fills my ears, even though there aren't any clocks in here, and I'm the only one who can hear them. My mum thinks I'm joking, but I'm really not, and I'm starting to wonder if there's something wrong with me.

Tick tock, tick tock, tick tock...

Hundreds of clocks seem to go off at once, and only in this room. Whatever is happening here is freaking me out. So much so that I've decided to never set foot in here again, but mum insisted I come up here and look for my own things, considering I'm almost thirteen.

Despite the radiator being on high, the air around me is icy cold, as if ghosts from the past are still hanging around. I think I could cope with a ghost encounter, but the ticking is driving me insane. Why am I the only one to hear it?

The room is full of my old toys and furniture we haven't sorted since moving to Wales a few months ago, and knowing my mother, this stuff will still be here in another few months, if not forever. She's a terrible hoarder, especially of antique books and broken furniture she says she'll upcycle but never gets around to.

The creaking and groans from the radiator make me jump out of my skin, so I try to hurry to find what I'm looking for.

Casting my eyes around the junk, I think I've found it. I lean over my old bike to reach the box that's precariously balanced on top of another box by the window, and I stumble forward, falling to my knees. Luckily, our old rug is there to cushion my fall and I pick myself up, coughing from the puff of dust that clouds around me. I half expected the dust to form the shape of a person standing next to me, as I certainly felt as though I was being watched, if not by someone behind the veil, maybe from somewhere in the distant universe. Although I read once about portals that take people to other dimensions, I'm sure they're just nonsense.

As usual, there is nothing but an empty space and my, "Wild, fanciful imagination," as Mum says. The box is labelled with a black marker. *Danny's WW2 replicas* and I open it, hoping to find my Second World War workbook for home education in the morning.

'Danny!' I hear my mother shouting from the back garden. I peer through the dusty, cracked windowpane to see Mum with her phone against one ear, waving at me.

'Did you find your books?' she hollers, standing in the downpour. She did a ridiculous version of The Time Warp, which made me laugh, but that's Mum, eccentric to the bone. Even though she's going through her own pain after Dad left, she always tries to make me laugh.

Mum is an archaeologist and historian, so waterlogged gardens are kind of her thing.

'Yeah, I've found it!' I shout back. *Miraculously.*

Being home educated isn't so terrible. It means I get to study topics I enjoy, and the Second World War is one of them. Our home has always been full of books and dinner-table conversations out the past, but when I get ask why I like that era, I can't explain it. I just am.

As I leave the room, the ticking gets louder and louder until an icy chill settles on my shoulders. I make a run for the door and bolt down the stairs, coming to a sudden halt on the bottom step. Standing in the hallway is a tall, broad-shouldered man wearing a long green wax coat and big, heavy black boots. He has a head full of grey, wispy hair, as though he had put a finger into an electric socket and got shocked. By his side is a small, white, scruffy dog who looks comical compared to the giant man.

'Um... Do I know you?' I ask, wondering why he's standing in our hallway, staring down at me rather rudely.

'I'm looking for your mam. Is she here?' he asks in a thick, friendly Welsh accent. He smiles, revealing a gap in his tooth. 'I'm Alfred Thomas, and this silly mutt is Jess,' he says as the dog cocks its head to the side. 'I hope you don't mind, but the door was open.' He gestures toward the open front door. Mum says we don't have to worry about locking up here, but I'm beginning to wonder. Outside our cottage is a sixteenth-century castle which occupies a wooded headland overlooking the sea. The courtyard is just yards from our front garden, and to the side of the cottage is a public footpath that leads to the cliffs behind us. The nearest neighbour is half a mile up the country road.

'Mum? Oh, she's out in the back garden, Mr Thomas. Shall I get her for you?' I relax, knowing he knows mum.

He furrows his brow at the book I'm holding and asks to see it. Flipping through the book with his thick, sausage fingers, he occasionally raises a brow at things that catch his eye. 'This is an interesting era. One of my favourites, too. I'm sure you'll like it here, kid,' he winks and hands me the book back. Just as I'm about to ask why, Mum walks through the kitchen door, dripping wet and covered in mud.

'Morning, Mr Thomas, is everything all right? I see you've met my boy, Danny,' she says, taking off her muddy wellingtons. 'You can call me Katherine, by the way.'

'Yes, I have, and please call me Alfred since we are practically neighbours.'

Mum offers him a chair. He sits down and pulls out a pile of files from inside his coat. 'I've brought you the information you wanted. I hope it is helpful, although I'm not sure what the local community will feel about digging up the old farmhouse, you see, it has been very well looked after over the years, considering its history.'

Mum flicks her sopping wet hair over her shoulder and sits down opposite Alfred. 'Pop the kettle on, Dan, would you mind?' she asks. 'Alfred, could I put in a request?'

I listen intently as I fill the kettle with cold water from the tap and then put it on the gas stove.

'You could try, but the owner of the land has passed away, and it has been left to the family.'

'Would you like tea, Mr Thomas?' I interject.

'I can't stay, sonny, maybe some other time,' he says. 'I've got errands to run in the castle, you see. I've been the caretaker for the last twenty years. My father was the caretaker before me, and his father before him. It's always busy, and now I have special visitors this week, you won't be seeing me about much.'

Alfred was about to stand up to leave when mum asks about the history of the area and the farmhouse.

He sits down again and says, 'Ah, the farmhouse. That was bombed during the war...' He rubs his chin. At the mention of the war, my ears perk up. 'That is a sad story, a sad story indeed. During the February Blitz in 1941, a German bomber, probably on its way back to HQ, dropped the rest of its bombs to save on fuel, or so we believe. Did you know that Swansea was bombed heavily because of its ports? The Germans blocked ships from coming in or out with food or weapons. It wasn't just London and the big cities that got destroyed, you know. Wales was hit, too. Well, anyway, one of those stray bombs landed on the farmhouse, killing all its occupants, including two lads, evacuees.'

'Oh my goodness,' exclaims Mum. 'I had no idea the story was so tragic.'

'It's sad indeed, Katherine. If only they could've been saved,' he says, and at that moment turns to face me and I realise for some reason that I feel responsible somehow, though I'm not sure why he made me feel like this. His whole demeanour changed in that instant. Mum, wrapped up in the story, doesn't notice.

'Oh dear, so sad. And so close to home,' she says, looking toward the kitchen window. 'I rather hoped I could get special permission to dig, since it's practically on our land. I would've liked to have written a paper on it.'

'A paper? Sounds interesting, but I am sure there are other ways to investigate.'

'Not really, no. Not when the internet isn't turning up much. I thought by digging up the ground, it might reveal personal things that could tell a story.'

'Well, I wish you luck in your endeavour,' he says, and at that moment, Alfred stands up and bids goodbye. 'I must be getting along. If there's anything else you need, I'm only a short walk away.' He tugs on Jess's lead and, as he passes me, winks, 'See you round, Danny Boy.' Nobody calls me that except for Gramps Norman and we're expecting him tomorrow.

Chapter Two

It's a chilly March. I wrap my scarf tightly around myself and close the kitchen door. Mum is kneeling by the back gate, painting it dark green. She found the tin of paint in the shed when we moved here, along with other things that have now found their way into the house, including a box of old files, a Bakelite radio, and a typewriter. All authentic and from the 1940s, much to my delight.

'Off exploring, are you?' she asks, looking up at me.

'I thought I'd go as far as the cliffs to take some pictures for Aunty Deb.'

Mum isn't very good at DIY, as the careless splotches on the flagstone path show.

'You missed a bit,' I say.

'Where?' She glances at her handiwork.

'Just there,' I point.

She leans closer to inspect the gate. 'Where? I don't see anything.'

'Just kidding, Mum. See you later,' I laugh and edge out the gate carefully to avoid getting paint on my jacket.

'Oh, you cheeky beggar,' she hollers back, 'and Happy Birthday, Dan, love you.'

'Thanks, Mum.'

Clutching my digital camera that hangs around my neck, I make my way onto the footpath beside our house, full of intrigue about the bomb Alfred told us about. Just as I'm about to push open the metal gate, I hear a car horn beeping and turn around.

'Happy Birthday, Danny Boy,' Grandad Norman shouts from the wound-down window.

Grandad Norman is Mum's dad and a professor of ancient history. I backtrack toward the house to greet him, and he gets out of the car and immediately pulls me into a bear hug.

'You're never too old for a hug from Gramps, eh, Dan?' He ruffles my hair. 'You've grown a few inches since I saw you last. Must be the Welsh air,' he laughs. 'Or maybe it's been a while since visits.'

Gramps has long, grey hair tied back into a ponytail and dresses as though it's still the 1950s.

'Probably both,' I say, waiting for him to give me my present. Gramps gives the best presents, probably because I'm his only grandchild.

'Oh yes, Happy Birthday.' He gets into the front seat of the car and opens the glovebox. 'I've been so busy lately, Dan, working and researching that you'll have to forgive my absence. I think what you're about to find out from my research will no doubt thrill you.' He hands me a carved wooden box that fits in my palm and tells me to open it. 'This is a family heirloom, and it must be looked after at all costs.'

'You mean it's an antique?' I was excited now, as I loved receiving anything old, apart from the latest video games, of course, but Gramps Norman hates those things and so I don't expect to get anything made in the last four decades, possibly five. But who knows with him, it may have come from out of space.

'Just open it!' he urges.

I lift the bronze latch and open the lid to find a dirty gold pocket watch on a chain.

'It belonged to my grandfather, Seamus,' he says. 'It's yours now, but it's not just any old pocket watch, you hear, so don't leave it lying around the place.'

'Thanks,' I say, taking it out of the box. It feels cold in my hand, and if I'm not mistaken, I feel a slight electrical shock too, but that's impossible. I look closely at the casing, noticing tiny planets carved into the gold. 'It's amazing, thank you. But why are you giving it to me?'

'It was meant for you, that's all.'

Just then he notices Mum by the gate and calls out, 'Kath, do you need a hand?'

As I was about to leave, Mum hollers, 'Too late, Dad, as usual. I've finished. Oh, and Dan, I'll text you when your party is ready.'

A party was the last thing I wanted, but I can't say anything as it makes her happy to organise it.

'Sure, Mum. I won't be long.'

I make my way onto the gravelly footpath bordered by hedges and bales of hay, toying with the pocket watch tucked in my jacket pocket. I hadn't come this far down the path before, since we'd only been here less than a week, and now in front of me was a fork in the road. From what I understood from the map I looked at before we came, one path led to the abandoned farmhouse at the end of our garden, and the other heads straight to the cliffs and steps that take you onto the beach. I decided to head to the cliffs as I wanted to take pictures. It was an overcast day, and the waves lap ferociously against the cliff face. There are no other people around, not even kids, in fact, I haven't met anyone my age since I'd been here. I snap some pictures and start heading back when I feel a slight vibration on the ground, quickly followed by a low drone of aircraft above my head. Glancing up, I inspect the sky but there's nothing but grey clouds scudding across, looking as though they're about to burst with rain. The drone becomes louder, and I find it peculiar that I can't see it, since it sounds as though it's right above my head. But then I feel a bubble of excitement in my belly when I recognised the sound of it. *It's a Spitfire!* 'It's a Spitfire!' I shout above the noise. I'd know that sound anywhere as they're my favourite planes. But what is it doing here? Disappointed I can't see it, I start my journey back home, beaming madly to myself that it appeared on my birthday of all days.

'Happy Birthday!' shouts Mum and Gramps as I walk through the kitchen door. They're both sitting at the kitchen table covered with a Union Jack tablecloth and plates of food. A Union Jack banner hangs across the wall and Mum has stuck a few of my WW2 propaganda posters on the kitchen cupboards.

'Did you have a nice walk, Dan? Did anything exciting happen?' Gramps asks whilst getting up from his chair to light the candles on the chocolate cake.

I shake off my jacket and drape it over the chair. 'A cow mooed in a field,' I laugh, thinking what a silly question. This is the countryside. 'Oh, I heard what I thought was a Spitfire flying above me, but I couldn't see it as dark clouds just came from nowhere, obscuring it.'

Gramps looks up at me mid-way through lighting the last of the five candles. I doubt Mum could find any more among the unpacked boxes. 'Really?' he asks, genuinely shocked. 'Are you sure it was a Spitfire? There's an airport not far away, you know.'

'Oh, how nice, Dan, a Spitfire flyover on your birthday. I take that as a lucky omen,' Mum says and begins piling my plate with food. If this is supposed to resemble a 1940s tea, I doubt very much they had Cadbury's chocolate fingers back then, but I'm not complaining. I gratefully take the plate from Mum and notice Gramps looking deep in thought while picking at a sausage roll.

'Dad, we haven't sung *Happy Birthday* yet,' she taps his hand. He snaps back to the present.

'Oh right, we haven't.'

Just as they're about to embarrass me, there's a tap at the door.

'Is it alright if I come in?' Alfred asks, with Jess following behind.

Gramps stands up. 'Good to see you, Alf. It's been a long time.' He shakes his hand and offers him a seat next to me.

'Ah, it's your birthday isn't it, Dan? Many happy returns of the day. Hey, I bet this will be a birthday to remember.' He sits down and pours himself a glass of squash. He doesn't notice the weird stare gramps is giving him. What is up with Gramps suddenly?

'So, here's to Danny,' Alf raises his plastic cup. 'Here's to a fabulous adventure of which I am sure there'll be many,' he says. Gramps still looks as though he could throttle him, and I have no idea why. I think it's hilarious. But what adventures? There's not much to do around here. More chance of World War Three happening.

After they sing *Happy Birthday*, Gramps and Alfred head out towards the castle where there are now many cars parked along the drive.

'What's going on over there?' I ask Mum, standing by the door and munching on pizza.

'Who knows, Dan? Alfred says he had important guests arriving, didn't he? Maybe it's some sort of convention or meet-up. I don't know what Dad is doing there, but he and Alfred have known each other for years. Anyway, time to clear up the mess,' she says and heads into the living room, leaving the dishes in the sink. Cleaning isn't Mum's favourite thing, so I make a start on clearing up.

'Night, Dan,' says Mum. I hear her bedroom door close, and I switch off my lamp. It's a clear night, so I sit up in bed and look out the window at the castle lit up from all angles. The cars were still parked outside, and I think about wandering over in the morning to find out what's going on there when I see two shadows approaching the cottage.

'It's all in motion now, Norm. There's nothing we can do but wait it out. He has the watch, which is the main thing. Let's hope he figures it out before it's too late,' says Alfred.

My stomach twists into a knot. *Why are they talking about me?* I pat my dressing gown pocket for the watch, but it isn't there. 'Oh no,' I feel my heart hammering in my chest and jump off the bed just as I hear *tick-tock-tick-tock-tick-tock* by my feet. I pick up the watch and open the casing to see both hands spinning around the clock face. This isn't normal. What is it about ticking clocks around here? I'm about to run downstairs to confront them both and ask what's going on when I'm stopped in my tracks by my bedroom door. There's a rustling of what sounds like papers being shuffled about in the back bedroom. I decide to crawl back into bed as there's nobody else in the house to make such a noise.

The next morning, while sitting at the kitchen table eating cornflakes, Gramps says he has extended his stay as he has business to attend to in the area. He wants to know if I'd help paint one of the spare rooms, as he has had enough of sleeping on the sofa.

'Not the back bedroom?' I ask, thinking of all the junk to remove.

'No, goodness no, not in there,' he says almost spluttering on his coffee.

I look at him curiously. 'Why not in there?' I ask, remembering the strange sounds I'd been hearing.

'Uh, claustrophobic, Dan. It's far too small. I thought I'd take the room next to yours. The walls haven't been painted since the 1950s, I believe. So, I think it's overdue for a bit of paint.'

'Yeah, definitely overdue,' I say and eat the rest of my soggy cornflakes. I want to ask him about his late-night conversation with Alfred I overheard, but I don't know how to raise the subject. I guess I shouldn't have eavesdropped in the first place.

'I'm just popping into town,' Mum says, walking into the kitchen. 'Do you need anything?'

I shake my head as I swallow a mouthful of food.

'Okay, see you later, then.'

'Bye, love,' Gramps hollers and immediately gets off the chair and heads out to the garden.

'Come on,' he yells, 'there's paint in here.'

The bedroom is about the same size as mine and overlooks the castle. Gramps gets into his white overalls and hands me a paintbrush. I'm busy painting the wall by the window when something catches Gramps' eye. He peers out the window and then makes an excuse about having something he must do.

'Carry on,' he says, and I hear his feet thundering down the stairs.

I look out the window, paintbrush in hand, when Alfred strolls up the path from the castle door and points toward the gate and then points toward his watch on his wrist. I can't make out what he's saying, but they both seem worried. As I'm about to add more paint to the wall, I hear the landing floorboards creaking as if someone is walking across them. 'Mum, are you back?' I shout, but there's no answer. Gramps is still talking to Alfred and there is nobody else here. I put the brush on the tin and head toward the bedroom door. 'Hello? Is anybody here?' I ask, stepping onto the landing. It's then that I hear a muffled conversation, and it sounds as though it's taking place in the back bedroom. *Not again.* I wonder what is going on. I tiptoe to the room and press my ear against the wooden door.

'You seem very distracted, Doctor. Is there somebody listening in?' a man says in a German accent.

I freeze outside the door and cover my mouth. My legs are now like jelly and I'm unable to move. Who is in the room? Just then the front door slams shut, and Gramps comes running up the stairs.

'Sorry about that, Dan. Have you finished?' he jokes, stopping dead on the landing, and looking at me as though I'm crazy.

'No, I haven't even started. I was just...' I don't know how to convey the truth because he would surely think I'd lost my marbles. 'Just had to find something, that's all,' I say and pat my pocket.

He looks at me curiously and I'm sure he doesn't believe a word. However, he says nothing, switches on an old Bakelite radio Mum found in the shed, and continues painting while whistling along to Vera Lynn's *We'll Meet Again*. I do a double take at the radio, thinking how odd that it's playing songs from the 1940s, and it's not even a digital radio.

Chapter Three

'It's time to get up lazy bones,' Mum hollers. I check the pocket watch, now ticking normally, and make my way downstairs. Mum is sitting at the kitchen table, head down in some paperwork. Gramps is nowhere to be seen.

'Where's Gramps?'

'He left early this morning. He says he has some stuff to sort out. Come and have a look at this,' she says. 'I got this from the local history web page.' She hands me a black-and-white photograph she printed out. 'Tell me what you see.'

'Two boys standing outside a cottage,' I say, then realise where it is. 'This is the farmhouse behind us, isn't it?'

Mum nods her head excitedly, her eyes lighting up for the first time in months. 'Yep, I'm researching the bomb explosion, but the internet isn't turning up much for some odd reason except for this photo. It's like nobody wants to remember it happened, or they're keeping it a secret. Strange, don't you think?'

'Yeah, it is a bit,' I agree, studying the photo. I notice someone at the back of the house by the fence. Although the image is slightly blurred, the person feels oddly familiar. I grab my magnifying glass from the kitchen drawer for a closer look. The image enlarges, but I can't make out any distinctive features; still, the person seems familiar. 'Can I keep this for a bit?' I ask, thinking a trip to the farmhouse is in order.

'If you want, Dan. I think I'm going to interview people around here, see if I can build a picture of what happened.'

'If they'll talk to you,' I say, wondering why Alfred and the community are very protective of the story and the site. 'I'm off for a walk, is that all right? I'll start schoolwork when I get back, I promise.'

'Make sure you do,' she says, 'or it's *War and Peace* again,' she chuckles.

I fold the picture and put it in my jacket pocket along with Gramps pocket watch and head out the door. The castle is quiet, not a visitor in sight, but then I see a piece of paper taped to the noticeboard saying the castle is closed until further notice.

About to head onto the path, a young couple with a baby in a pram say hello and head through the gate. I wave back, and when I reach the gate to open the bolt, the family is nowhere to be seen. I think it's weird how quickly they've reached the bend in the path. Not even I can walk that fast. I lock the gate behind me and feel an electrical charge surge through my body. I freeze on the other side of the gate and shake my head, confused. 'Weird,' I say and walk toward the fork in the path. I take the left turn and head toward the farmhouse when I hear what sounds like children laughing. I think it might be the couple I saw earlier. Maybe they had more kids with them who rushed ahead. Just then, out of nowhere, a white paper aeroplane swoops out of thin air and lands at my feet.

'Pass us our plane,' a voice says in a cockney accent.

I'm still staring at the plane when I see two sets of bare feet also standing in front of me. I look up and see two boys who look familiar looking back at me. The taller one, about my age and has thick, dark curly hair and curious, bright green eyes. The other, probably around seven, with a mop of blonde hair, a dirty face, and a scowl, crosses his arms and urges the older one to beat me up.

'Woah, I come in peace,' I say, stooping to pick up the plane. I'm about to hand it back to the younger boy when I notice what they're wearing. Grey tank tops and black shorts. The first thing I think of is the picture tucked in my pocket. But it's not possible.

'Who are you?' the younger boy asks rudely.

'Who are *you*?' I reply, stunned by his cheek.

'Don't think you're taking our plane,' the younger one replies. 'Go on, Francis, sort him out.'

'Shut up, Jack,' the older boy scolds. 'You shouldn't talk to strangers. What did Mum tell you before we left, eh? Besides, careless talk costs lives, doesn't it? Who knows where he comes from?'

The younger boy continues to stare at me, and I find it really unnerving. *What is his problem?*

'What do you mean by where I come from? I live...' I was about to point to the cottage when something stops me from revealing too much. What I'm experiencing doesn't feel normal, for some reason. 'I'm just a kid like you,' I say. 'I'm not a threat to anyone. By the way, my name is Danny.'

'You're dressed oddly for around here,' Francis says. 'Where do you live again?'

'He talks funny, too. Doesn't he talk funny, Francis?' Jack tugs at the older boy's sleeve, but he pays him no attention. He continues to stare at me like I'm an alien who has just landed on a spaceship.

At this point, I don't know what to say, so I decide the truth is better. At least I won't put my foot in it any further. I point in the direction of the cottage. 'I didn't say where I lived but if you must know it's just by the castle,' I say.

'Oh yeah, sure about that?' Francis says. I have no idea why he says this, and I don't think to ask why because now I see the farmhouse, complete with every brick, window, and slate attached to its roof. My eyes pop at the sight. How is this happening? I step back, about to run home when a woman comes out of the door and calls the boys to come and get their dinner.

'We'd better go,' says Francis. 'Are you all right? You look as if you've seen a ghost,' he says, standing there as Jack runs back to the house. 'Or maybe you're the ghost, who knows?'

'A ghost? What do you mean?' I mutter. He then turns and runs back to the farmhouse while I bolt back down the path, my head reeling with a billion thoughts.

As I reach the gate, I feel the electric charge once more and hear the incessant ticking of the watch in my pocket. I yank it out as I run toward the kitchen door and look at it. The hands are spinning like crazy. Did this have anything to do with what just happened? Nah, I think it's just a stupid watch. *Or is it?* Grandad dealt with strange, ancient objects in his line of work, so who knows where this comes from, or to whom it belonged?

I burst through the kitchen door, slamming straight into Mum carrying a box, the contents of which fly into the air and scatter all over the floor.

'What has got into you?' she asks, rolling her eyes at the mess.

'Nothing,' I mutter, gathering up the papers. 'What's all this?'

'While you were skiving off, I was going through the stuff in the shed and found these very interesting files. But that's not all, look,' she retrieves something from her trouser pocket and hands it to me. 'I had a sneaky dig at the top end of our field. It's a German officer badge, isn't it?'

I study the small silver badge in my hand and nod. This is unbelievable. I think about telling her what had happened at the farmhouse, but I don't know how to put it into words - I can't believe it myself.

'Look, look,' she squeals with excitement, shoving a folder into my hands. 'Read it.'

The yellowed, faded paper is written in German with an official-looking heading. 'I can't read German very well,' I say. 'We stopped lessons to learn Latin, remember? Do you know what it's about?'

'Something about a Doctor Fritz. My German is rusty, too. Maybe we ought to wait and ask Gramps. I wish he'd catch up with the modern world and buy a mobile phone.'

While Mum goes to the local shop for something for our tea, I sit in the living room on a comfortable, yet faded red sofa, trying to come to terms with all that's happened lately. There's the Spitfire, the two boys, a Doctor Fritz, and a German officer badge. None of it makes sense, let alone the farmhouse looking as though it had just been built. The house is silent for once, and there is no *ticking* or *tocking* to annoy, but I think I may have spoken too soon as the pocket watch begins to *tick* erratically, as though it's trying to get my attention.

'I need to go back to the farmhouse,' I say aloud. I need to see if the boys weren't a figment of my imagination, so I run upstairs to my room to collect my rucksack, thinking I'd take them a chocolate cake to be friendly, and cross the hallway to my room. About to push open my bedroom door, I turn to the back room at the end of the hall, sure I hear something rustling. It's either rats or, worse, someone is in there. Walking across the creaky landing, the sound of *ticking* gets louder and louder. I take a sharp breath and reach my hand out to push open the door when there's a crash and someone, very faintly, cursing under their breath. In German! I push the door open, expecting the worst, and see nothing but our pile of rubbish from the last house.

'Weird, just weird,' I whisper, stepping into the room to inspect every corner. I don't hang around and run out the door and down the stairs just as Mum pulls up in the car.

'Mum is it alright if I take the leftover cake?' I'm already wrapping it in foil before she can answer.

'Yeah, of course, Dan. If you'll wait until I put all this food away, I'll cook us a proper dinner,' she says, unloading groceries onto the kitchen counter. 'Why do you need all that anyway?' she looks at the great lump I sliced.

'I think I saw a couple of kids on the farm,' I say, not wanting to give specific details just yet. I still don't know if they are real.

'Oh, did you?' she exclaims. 'That's nice. Course you can take it. Just make sure they're not allergic to any of the ingredients as I don't want their parents at my door.'

I thought there was no way it would happen, not if they're from the 1940s.

'Will do. I'll see you later,' I say, and I'm out the kitchen door and up the garden path before I hear her shout, 'Love you,' like she always does, followed by, 'We'll go through the bits I found later, yeah?'

'All right, Mum,' I yell as I head towards the gate.

About to slide the bolt, I glance back at the castle and see Alfred chatting with a couple of men outside the main door. He looks over for a split second but doesn't acknowledge me, so I wave, yet he still doesn't respond. *Rude.* I walk through the gate, close it, and hear the roar of aircraft above me, so loud, I cover my ears. I look up to see Hurricanes and Spitfires flying overhead that weren't there a second ago. Mesmerised by the swathe of planes that look like giant silhouetted birds in the sky, I don't hear my name being called until I feel a slight tug at the sleeve on my elbow.

'Jack?' I say, and the little boy steps back, grinning. Just then I see Francis running up the path toward us, glancing worriedly at the planes as he does so. This don't look good. And the planes weren't here a few seconds ago when I was at the other end of the gate. What on earth just happened? I must look freaked out as Francis shakes me so hard to get my attention.

'Danny?' he shouts. 'There's a war going on, you know. There's no time for panic, we must get on with it. The planes fly over most days and nights.'

'Where are they going?' I ask, wondering if I'd stumbled into the Battle of Britain or some other historic event of the war.

'Eh? I don't know, they're probably training for something. There's a base a few miles away. You'd know that if you lived over there,' he points towards the castle.

I think I've been caught out, and now I don't have a backup story to give. How could I tell the truth when I don't know the truth, either?

Just then Jack thumps his arm. 'Come on, Francis, we'll be late for school.'

'Yeah, we'd better go,' says Francis. 'Are you going to school, too?' he asks.

We walk towards the gate and I'm inwardly freaking out in case they see me disappear or something.

'Sort of, yeah. I learn at home, with my billeting family,' I say, rather unconvincingly.

'It's alright, Danny, we know,' Francis says, tapping a hand on my shoulder with a smug grin. 'What do you know?' I ask as beads of sweat begin to form across my forehead.

Jack runs ahead, shouting they'll be late if they don't hurry, and Francis doesn't answer my question. I'm sure he knows something.

'Oh, here, before I forget,' I say, hoping to change the subject. I dig into my rucksack for the cake and produce a big lump of shiny foil. Francis looks at it as though it's dropped from outer space.

'What the heck is that?' he asks, and even Jack comes running back to inspect it.

'So pretty,' he says, 'like a big lump of silver. Is it silver?' Jack says, reaching out to grab it.

'No, it's a cake, and the silver is foil. I got the chocolate from... America,' I say, wondering if the Americans had entered the war yet. 'My aunt lives there,' I lie, feeling guilty. I unwrap the foil and their mouths drop wide open.

'It's just cake,' I tell them. 'I brought it for you as it was my birthday yesterday.'

'Blimey, where did you get this?' Francis asks. 'Not sure if there are enough rations for one slice, let alone a whole cake.'

I didn't think this through at all. The cake was certainly extravagant, if not a luxury in this day and age. 'Oh, we have chickens for eggs, and we make our own butter,' I say, I realising I don't know half of what I'm talking about and better shut up and get home. The gate is a few yards away and my mouth is so dry it's like scratchy sandpaper.

'Lovely cake,' Jack enthuses, 'probably the best I've ever had,' he says, with a mouth full of cake.

'Me too,' says Francis, stopping directly in front of the gate. 'But we'd better not tell Mrs Granger that,' he laughs. 'She's the best baker in the village.'

'Or so she says,' Jack bursts out laughing.

I take a deep breath, relieved they don't ask more awkward questions.

'See that cottage,' Francis points toward my home, barely visible through the thick hedge. I see the slate roof and chimney and the tip of the back bedroom window. I can hardly believe I'm standing here looking at it from the past. 'Strange things go on in there,' he says, and now I'm curious. What could he know? 'The owner is German, we're sure of it. He has a German name, but he sounds very English,' he goes on. 'His name is Fritz. We don't see him much as he prefers to keep to himself.'

FRITZ! I'm blown away and I can barely contain my excitement, but it also takes me by surprise as I thought Seamus owned it. Then I realise something I hadn't thought of before - I could meet my great-great-grandfather! I could even solve the family mystery!

'We'd better go,' Francis says, 'or we'll be late. See you later Danny, and thanks for the cake.' They're about to close it behind them when Francis hollers, 'And Happy Birthday.'

'Thanks, and no problem. See you again,' I say, watching them until they were out of sight. Now they're gone, I take another look at the house and notice a dark shadow passing the bedroom window and hear the faint *ticking* of a clock. *What is it about clocks and this house? Even in the 1940s!*

I loiter by the gate, staring at the figure pacing about the room, scratching their head as if thinking deeply about something. Whomever it is seems agitated. Just then, they stop right in front of the window, and the next thing I know, the window is being pushed open and a man with dark hair sticks his head out and makes eye contact with me. It was time to get home, so I make a dash through the gate, my heart pounding like crazy. *Did he see me? What if he did?*

Chapter Four

For a small dog, Jess's growl is fierce. So fierce, in fact, that I'm actually scared of her right now. She's standing outside the gate, growling madly at me, and I wonder what I've done to deserve such a reaction. I turn to lock the gate behind me and sidestep around her when, out of nowhere, Alfred walks toward me, telling Jess to calm down.

'What's got into you, eh?' He scoops her up into his arms, yet she still stares at me with her teeth bared as though I were some kind of monster. 'Sorry about that, Dan. I don't know what's got into her. So, where have you been?' he asks, which almost sounds accusatory.

'Oh, I just went for a stroll, you know,' I shrug. 'Have you seen Gramps by any chance?'

'He's around... somewhere,' Alfred says, and I feel like he is hiding something from me, but I don't know what. He's giving the impression he knows more than he's letting on, I'm sure of it.

It's then I hear the *ticking* of the pocket watch and thrust my hand into my pocket to block out the noise, but Alfred's keen ears and sharp eyes are already latched onto it.

What do you have there?' he asks, nodding toward the pocket.

'It's just a present from Gramps. I must be getting along now, Alfred. Mum has dinner on.'

My head feels spaced out by all that has happened, so I saunter towards my cottage, aware Alfred is still standing with Jess and staring at me. Why, I don't know. He can't know what just happened, can he?

I'm relieved to see the house is as I know it, with the freshly painted green fence and a new hanging basket of pink flowers by the door that wasn't there earlier. The front door is open a touch, so I push it and step inside, calling for Mum.

'Kitchen, Dan. You've been gone an awfully long time. Did you make friends, then?' She turns from the oven and hands me a large bowl filled with pasta topped with grated cheese.

'Yeah, they're cool, really nice. From London, I think.'

'Oh, you have something in common already, then. Sit down, I have news you're going to want to hear.'

I think it can't be as exciting as what just happened to me, but sit down anyway and tuck into my meal. I stuff the pasta in my mouth, surprised at how hungry I am. Time travel is hard work.

'I have a friend who speaks German, and she translated some of the documents for me. Apparently, it's a deed that says that this house is owned by a Doctor Fritz who bought it for a few hundred pounds. Dan, that means that in the early 1940s this house wasn't owned by Seamus. Isn't that a surprise? I always thought he lived here during the war; I think Dad will know more, but how exciting.'

'Have you researched Doctor Fritz?' I ask, thinking about the shadow I saw in the bedroom and what the boys told me.

'Not yet. There's so much to do and uncover here.'

After I wolf down the last of the pasta, I rush upstairs to my room, but as I reach the top of the landing, I hear voices again, in German.

I'm also struck by the sound of clocks and feel annoyed there could be someone else in the house. I run to the door and push it open with such force that the door slams against the doorstop, making a loud racket. Yet, it doesn't disturb the three gentlemen sitting around a large wooden desk piled high with folders stuffed with papers.

'Oh my god!' I shout, frozen to the spot, yet they don't stir or even acknowledge my presence. *What the hell is going on?* Slowly, but surely, I take in the room, the clocks on the wall covering every inch, the two men sitting crossed-legged at the end of the desk close to me. They are German and are speaking about the Fuhrer. The man behind the desk, listening but seemingly uncomfortable, has jet-black hair and a thin moustache. He's wearing a white lab coat and can't be any older than thirty. I'm sure at one point he looks at me pleadingly for help, but I can't be sure if it wasn't just my imagination. What am I seeing here? A residual energy? Another time vortex or what?

'Doctor, the Fuhrer needs your co-operation in this matter. It's why we have given you three months in which to complete our request. I am not at liberty to say because this is top class secret, but there are plans to invade Poland soon. If our plans should fail,' he chuckles, 'and that's a very big IF, we will need a backup plan. So, you see why this project is very important to the Fuhrer in order to reach his long-term goals.'

There is an uncomfortable pause, and Doctor Fritz levels his eyes to mine. Now I am certain he knows I'm here, but how I don't know.

Doctor Fritz takes a handkerchief from his trouser pocket and dabs his brow. 'Speaking freely, if I may, gentlemen. Despite my reservations about Hitler and the fact that I am being forced to do this, I would like it clearly stated on record that you approached me about my work and not the other way around. Do we have an agreement?'

The German closest to me tapped his fingers on his brown leather briefcase resting on his lap and nodded. 'Okay, as long as you complete the project in time and let us know when it's safe to arrange a collection.'

My ears can't believe what they're hearing. I slowly back out the door, hand on the doorknob and close it behind me, when I notice Doctor Fritz's eyes boring into mine as though he is trying to communicate something with me. Then, just as I am about to shut it tightly, the silence is broken by the front door opening and closing, and the scene before me disappears as though someone had switched the television off, and the room is filled with our junk again.

I slam the door closed and stand outside the bedroom door, shaking and breathing heavily, thinking I need to find out who Fritz is and what he is a doctor of.

Whatever I had witnessed, I know one thing for sure: it had to be stopped. The thought of Hitler having a secret weapon to win the war makes me sick and nervous. Sitting at my desk, I'm feeling irritated that the internet returns no results for Doctor Fritz. Just then, Mum comes into the bedroom with a mug of cocoa and a plate of biscuits. 'Here you go, thought you may be hungry,' she says, leaning over my shoulder. 'What are you looking for?'

'Doctor Fritz, but what do you know? There's nothing on the net about him and nothing in the local history book I've read about twenty times.' I lean back in my chair and cross my arms in annoyance.

She sits on the bed and nicks a biscuit from my plate. 'It's weird, isn't it?' she mumbles, spitting biscuit crumbs all over my bed. 'How can there be nothing at all? Someone around here must remember him or at least know of him. It's all getting rather odd, isn't it?' She ruffles my hair and gets up to leave. 'Oh, Gramps is downstairs, go and ask him. If he doesn't know, then I don't know what else to suggest except going back to the past to find out.' She closes the door and I'm shaken by her words.

What a weird thing to say considering the day I've had. But maybe she is right - maybe I need to go back to the past for answers. First, I need to talk to Gramps. He knows this house better than anyone but thinking about how Mum and I came to own it seems strange now. The cottage hadn't been lived in for a couple of decades, and as soon as Mum divorces, Gramps more or less threw the keys at her saying it would be a new start for us both and that it was imperative we move in as soon as possible. Why the urgency?

'Gramps,' I say, stepping into the front room. He's sitting in his chair reading the local newspaper. 'I need to ask you something important.'

He lowers the paper enough to see him raise a brow. 'Oh yeah?'

'Yeah,' I reply and flop onto the sofa. 'Tell me the story about Seamus.' I thought I'd get to the point, no-nonsense. Something tells me that time is very significant here, what with the ticking clocks and the pocket watch.

He clears his throat and slowly lowers the paper to his lap. 'Seamus Jones, my grandfather?'

'Well, yeah. I don't know any other Seamus Jones, do you?'

He frowns. 'No, I don't.'

'Then what's the story? What made him a legend in the war? Or wasn't he a legend, and it's all made-up nonsense?'

He shifts about uncomfortably in his chair, folds the paper, and takes a deep breath.

'I knew this day would come,' he says, more to himself than to me. 'Dan, I can only tell you what you need to know. Do you understand? Do not go asking me questions that I am not at liberty to answer, okay?'

'I think...' Even more confused than before, I shrug.

He gets up off the chair and sits down next to me and suddenly I feel this is getting rather serious. I wonder if I should tell him I can time travel, but I decide to wait until he finishes what he needs to tell me first.

'It is said that Seamus is... *was* a very important man. Probably more important than Winston Churchill at the time, but don't let him know I said that - I mean, what am I talking about?' he laughs nervously. I wonder what is wrong with him. Didn't Churchill die in the 1950s? 'Anyway, he was involved in, let's say *something* that affected the outcome of the war, and if it weren't for his bravery, we wouldn't be here now. However, something unfortunate happened on the night of this heroic deed that could reverse history. Mad as it sounds, Dan, something is still very much happening right now, under our noses, which could change everything, and I do mean *everything*.' At this moment, he looks directly into my eyes to emphasise the seriousness of it all. It alarms me a bit as I wasn't expecting such a dramatic conversation. I nod, my mouth agape.

'Okay, so...' I think about my next question carefully, but decide I have nothing to lose at this point. 'Does this something has anything to do with the pocket watch?' I ask subtly, hoping he will answer so I can tell him about time travelling.

'It does and I don't think I need to tell you what it's capable of either as I think you've already figured that out for yourself.'

My head feels woozy with the confirmation that I wasn't dreaming it nor am I going mad. 'Danny, listen to me. Careless talk still costs lives, and that's why I can't divulge much more now. I have my own problems to deal with, which you will no doubt find out about when it's time. You will figure this story out for yourself because you must.' He puts a firm hand on my shoulder, and I begin to feel the gravity of the situation, even if I am not sure what the situation is at the moment. I nod. 'And Doctor Fritz?' I ask.

'You've met... I mean, you've learned about him too, haven't you?'

'Sort of. I can't find anything on the internet. Who is he?'

'Someone important. He owned the house before my father, and that's all I can tell you, Dan. I can't risk saying anything else because it might affect the outcome, but know that I'll be around watching.'

My head is pounding now as I know that I did time travel back to the 1940s, but for what reason and how I must find out. Gramps gets up off the sofa and leaves the room, asking if I want a sandwich, but I can't think about eating now that I have discovered all this information. It was then I notice a thick hardback book on the table titled: *Day to Day Guide to the Second World War*, and I snatch it up for some bedtime reading.

Chapter Five

Adog barks, which can only mean Jess is running around the courtyard. I push aside my curtains to see a solitary light on at the castle. Alfred has been quiet the last couple of days and I'm wondering what his involvement is in all of this. The pocket watch strikes 10:00 p.m., so I grab my jacket from my desk and head downstairs.

Closing the kitchen door quietly, I step out into the cool, but clear night and walk toward the castle. Jess soon sniffs me out and comes running up to me.

'Hey girl, be quiet for a minute, okay?' I whisper, making my way along a shadowy path. Just then, the door to the castle opens and two men wearing ARP uniforms emerge. I back into the hedge so as not to be seen and crouch down, holding Jess, praying she doesn't give me away.

'What a nightmare this is, isn't it?' says one to the other. I can't make out who they are, but what on earth are they wearing ARP uniforms for? ARP means Air Raid Precautions. During the war, many civilians were assigned to patrol the streets, making sure people turned their lights off in their houses and used blackout blinds. It was to confuse the enemy so they couldn't see where they were going and drop bombs. Many ARP wardens also assisted when places were bombed and were trained in disposing of them, too. It was an important job. Anyway, nothing makes sense right now.

'Aye,' says the other, 'as soon as that lad closes the gate for good then we can all relax,' he slurps on his drink. 'God, sometimes I feel like this has dragged on forever.'

'What are you standing about for?' a voice booms from the doorway. It's Alfred, and he is livid. 'Get back in here now. We have a lot of work to do this evening and do keep it down out there. Walls have ears, you know, and so do thirteen-year-old kids.'

The two men say nothing but step back inside. Alfred looks around, checking for who knows what, and closes the door behind him.

'Gate?' I whisper. I look over at the gate beside our house and wonder if he means that gate, but then, I always close it after me so what did he mean by closing it for the final time?

I leave Jess go and run back to the cottage, stopping inches from the door. Maybe I should pay the past another visit, but then I see I'm wearing pyjamas and decide to find suitable clothing.

There's no sound from the room at the end of the hallway, thankfully, so, with caution, I turn the door handle and slam the light switch on. However, I can relax since this time there are no Germans around, just the junk and a box which has fallen from the pile. I notice papers and files fanned out across the floor that weren't there earlier and immediately get on my knees to inspect them. If I'm not mistaken, Mum brought them in from the shed.

Stamped in big, bold letters, is *Top Secret*. Excited, I flip it open, but it is in German. Argh! Why did I choose Latin? Mum had given me the choice to learn a new language last year and to be clever I said Latin, not expecting her to order all the learning materials that evening. Therefore, I had no choice but to stick with it. Although, I don't regret it because it's cool to speak a dead language, especially when I go to the shops for Mum, and it confuses the shopkeeper when I say hello. They always ask where I come from! But I can work out the date and it reads 11th February 1941. The date rings a bell, though. I scrambled through all my history lessons in my head and I'm pretty sure it was the date of the Blitz. Why would Fritz have letters about the Blitz. Why would Fritz have letters about the Blitz and why would Seamus not throw them out when he owned the cottage? Figuring it was relevant somehow to my investigation into what was going on here, I fold up the paper and stuff it in my pocket.

I don't have to look far when I glance up and see my box of old clothes. Yep, Mum doesn't even throw away clothes.

I throw on an old grey jumper and a pair of black trousers that shouldn't raise questions and creep across the landing, checking in on Mum who is snoring, and close the door.

For the first time, I'm actually nervous about walking through the gate and I don't know if it's because of what I've learned or whether it's dawning on me what I can do. Either way, I need to snap out of this and find my courage because it sounds like I'm doing important work, even though I don't know what it is I'm supposed to be doing.

I push the gate and shiver uncontrollably. The night is cool, and the path ahead is just black, with no light from anywhere but a sliver of moonlight through a lonesome cloud passing across it. Remembering the words of the men outside the castle earlier, I close the gate, still unsure what they meant. Then, the sky gradually gets lighter and lighter until I can see planes zooming across a brilliant blue sky.

Making my way along the path, I feel my heart beating in my chest. Even though I really don't like the feeling of having the responsibility on my shoulders, I continue to the farmhouse, unsure of what I'll find there. The first thing I need to know is what is the date and maybe from that, I can work out the rest. Hopefully. I'm nearing the farmhouse and where there is rubble in my world, here the house is whole. I still find it difficult to believe.

About to walk up the well-trodden path to the house, I hear someone whispering my name.

I turn sharply to my left and see Jack and Francis crouched behind the hedge.

'What are you doing?' I ask.

'Come 'ere,' says Francis. 'See them?' he points.

I peek over the hedge and see the land girls who volunteered to help with the Dig for Victory effort. Because all the men had been sent to fight, the women did most of their jobs and these women were making sure that people had enough to eat.

'We've got to get past them,' says Francis.

'Why?' I ask.

'To get to the oddball's cottage at the other end,' Francis says, and smirks at me. 'You know about the cottage, don't you?'

'Yeah,' I nod, not sure what he's getting at.

'Strange things go on in there. Come and see.' He waves me over to follow his lead through a gap in the hedge. 'Misery guts farmer Hughes won't be pleased, so we'd better be careful and not get spotted.'

I see there are about seven women who will spot us, and I don't like our chances of being invisible across an expansive open field. 'Okay, count me in,' I say.

Jack gets into position for the sprint. He scrunches his face in concentration, and I laugh out loud.

'On three,' Francis says, 'one, two, and three...'

We race across the field as fast as our legs can carry us. Surprisingly, Francis is in the lead, and I notice the land girls I've read books about are actual real-life people. I mean, of course they were real people but now they were really in front of me.

'Hey, Francis where are you off to?' a young woman in a green jumper and beige trousers shouts. 'You know you're not supposed to be on the field,' she chuckles. 'He will have your guts for garters.' She turns to her friend, tapping her on the shoulder and they both laugh at us as we sprint the last few yards. Jack crawls under the fence first, and then Francis.

'Is this a good idea,' I ask. 'We don't know what this guy is capable of?'

Francis laughs it off. 'Yes, we do, future boy.'

'What did you just say?' I ask but am interrupted by a loud mechanical sound coming from the upstairs window - the dreaded back bedroom. I turn to Francis, but he's gone! I turn the other way and see him by the front door about to turn the handle.

'Is this wise?' I ask, in a hoarse whisper, checking around to see if nobody else is lurking. 'By the way, why did you say future?' And then he is in the cottage.

'Come on, it's fine, we've done this many times.'

I step onto the concrete slab path, the same one I walked on seventy-odd years into the future, and it feels weird, almost surreal. 'Are you sure...?' I ask, but he disappears into the house. My throat feels dry all of a sudden and I was dreading what I'll find. As soon as I step over the threshold, I hear the tick, tick, ticking of clocks, but this time I see them too, hundreds of clocks adorning the hallway walls. Cuckoo clocks, tall grandfather clocks, and pocket watches on a sideboard of many shapes and sizes.

'Pssst, over here,' Francis whispers, and I snap out of my thoughts and follow him into the kitchen. I'm not prepared for what I was about to see, and my mouth drops at the amount of watch parts there are piled on the kitchen table. Springs and coils in amongst a plethora of notebooks and files. What is this man's obsession with clocks about? I knew I had to find out.

'What are we doing here?' I whisper.

'Looking for clues,' he replies, sifting through the notebooks on the table.

'But why?' I ask, really wanting to get out of here.

'There are rumours he's a spy for the Germans. I hear Mr Crompton; the ARP warden, say they have suspicions about him. Imagine if we caught him fraternising with the enemy, we'd be heroes.'

Suddenly, something makes sense, but Gramps claims he's important, but no threat was implied. At least he doesn't make him sound like a threat to our national security. I don't know what to think of this when I hear the floorboards creak above us.

'Come on, it's not worth it. If we get caught...'

'Keep your hair on,' Francis says coolly.

'If there's anything incriminating, we would've seen it by now.' At that moment, I remember the document I found in the attic in German. Now I'm not quite sure.

'See, even you're curious as to what's going on here, aren't you?'

He stuffs papers down his jumper and urges me out of the kitchen into the living room.

'Why all these clocks?' I ask.

'Do you want to know what the clocks are for?' he asks sheepishly.

'Yeah, but what if he catches us?' I panic.

'Nah, he's busy working on his experiment, he usually is at this time of day. Me and Francis worked it out, here,' he hands me a hardback book.

I turn it over. *The Theory of Time Travel* by Doctor L.M Fritz. The pocket watch suddenly feels heavy in my pocket and the room begins to spin with all this new information. But what did all this have to do with me? If he has created a time travelling device, then it could only mean that the pocket watch was created by him, but for what purpose? It was then we hear someone coming down the stairs.

Chapter Six

We're almost across the field when I see a vexed man with a red face running toward us. I think it's the angry farmer. as the land girls are laughing and pointing at us.

'You'd better run, boys,' they yell, and I just make it through the gap in the fence when I notice the exasperated farmer bending over, gasping for breath. Phew! That was a close one.

'You might as well come in for a drink,' says Francis, slightly out of breath. 'Come on. Mrs Granger makes a delicious lemonade.'

'Mrs Granger?' I ask as I followed him to the back door.

'She's our 'evacuee "Mum" as Jack calls her.'

I follow Francis into the kitchen, where the smell of cooking meat fills the air. A wooden table is occupied by two men in local defence uniforms, hunched over bowls of soup. The Local Defence Volunteers, or the Home Guard they came to be known, consisted of volunteers between the ages of seventeen and sixty-five who were exempt from normal military service. The younger man still wore his armband with LDV stitched on it.

'All right, boys, sit your butts down,' the older man says with a flick of his spoon. The other man, younger, maybe in his twenties, with slicked-back hair full of hair gel, holds the spoon close to his mouth. 'And you are?' he asks me.

'Danny, sir. Pleased to meet you.' I extend my hand.

He puts down his spoon and shakes my hand with a firm grip. 'The same goes for you, sonny. New around here?'

'Yeah, sort of,' I say. 'We moved here from London a week ago.'

'Another Londoner, is it?' says a woman walking through the hallway. She has curly red hair and a kind, round face. I recognised her instantly as the woman who called the boys for dinner.

Mrs Granger shuffles into the kitchen and claps her eyes on me. 'Oh, you're the boy they've been talking about, aren't you?' She pulls me in for a hug.

'Yes, Mrs. Granger. Nice to meet you.'

'And you. I'm glad the boys have someone to play with. They've been terribly lonely. Well, I hope you're hungry.' She then looks at the young man sitting at the table. 'Seamus, if you've finished, give the boy the chair.'

SEAMUS! It can't be. I unintentionally stare at the man who may just be my great-great-grandfather. I see my mother's eyes staring back at me and feel as though I'm about to pass out from shock when Francis clicks his fingers in front of my face. This brings me back to reality. But is this reality? I don't even understand what's happening anymore.

'Your soup,' he says, and Seamus got up, ruffles my hair, and walks to the sink.

'The chair is all yours,' Seamus says.

I take my seat opposite the older man, who seems to have pressing matters on his mind. Grunting a hello, he slurps the contents of the bowl.

'This is my husband, Sidney,' says Mrs Granger. 'Ignore his filthy habits. He's one of the Home Guards around here.'

'Nice to meet you, sir.'

'You too.' He gets up from the chair and puts the bowl in the sink. 'We're on watch tonight, Seamus so don't forget the damn binoculars this time.'

Seamus nudges my arm. 'Don't worry. No Germans are about to land on the beach tonight or any other night. Not while we're on watch, isn't that right, Sid?'

'That's right, lad, so don't any of you worry. I'd be more worried about that oddball in the next cottage,' he spits, and a piece of carrot he'd been chewing flies out across the table.

A German invasion was the least of my worries, but I can't tell him that - or could I? My head is a whirlwind of questions right now as I look down at the thin, watery liquid with two pieces of grey meat, a potato, and a carrot bobbing back up at me. I scoop a spoonful under the watchful eye of Francis.

'It's not that terrible, you know. Or is food better where you come from?'

I glance curiously at Francis. 'What do you mean?'

'Even your cakes are better.' He smirks and shrugs his shoulders before dipping a hunk of bread into his bowl.

Have I been caught out? He can't possibly know about my time travelling, or could he? I mean, the house is practically overlooking ours, so he may have seen me appearing at the gate.

'Hey, you lot, if you haven't got much to do, there's a shed out the garden that needs clearing. We need it for a shelter in case of... well, in case of anything really,' he says, looking at Jack's worried expression. 'A bob in it for each of you,' says Sidney as he leaves through the back door with Seamus. 'And you, Danny.'

'Thank you, Mr Granger.'

As I turn back, I notice a folded newspaper on the empty chair. I pick it up and check the date. February 9th, 1941. Two days until the Blitz! I really thought I had longer than this, but since I don't, I need to think - fast!

'You all right, Dan? It's just a newspaper.' Francis says, beckoning me out the door. 'What's got you so worried there?' he asks, and I wish he wasn't so observant.

'Just the war, I guess,' I shrug and followed him out into the back garden.

'I'm not going in there,' Jack says, folding his arms across his chest. 'There'll be all sorts of bugs.' He scrunches up his face. I think to myself that it's better than a German pursuing a time-travelling device, but don't say anything.

Francis hands him a pair of gloves. 'You're doing as you're told, Jack. If Mum were here, she'd make you.' He thrusts the gloves toward Jack, who reluctantly puts them on, even though they're about two sizes too big.

Jack's eyes fill with tears. 'But she isn't, is she?' he stomps. 'She's stuck in London, and we might not see her again. The man on the radio says...'

'Stop listening to the radio, then,' Francis scolds, but then softens. 'It's a war, Jack. Nasty stuff happens, all right? But we are here in the country and we're safe. And Mum has a shelter at the end of her road, so she'll be fine.'

I kneel beside Jack. 'Listen, Jack, it's really important that we clear the shed, okay? It's for our safety, like Mr Granger says. So, let's make it a game, shall we? The first person to haul out the most can get my bob off Mr Granger.'

'Really!' Francis is shocked. 'You rich or something?'

I turn to him and wink. 'No,' I whisper, 'but it'll be a fun game, right?'

'Right, if you say so,' Francis nods unconvincingly and pulls on a pair of gloves.

' Okay, let's see what's in this shed,' I say, approaching the paint-peeling door.

I take the plunge, open the door, and step back in case of a German onslaught. Instead, rusty old shovels and rakes fall out into the muddy ground. Thank goodness for that. We get on with emptying the shed, and I have a strange feeling that this will be meaningful somehow.

After about an hour, I stand up straight and wipe the sweat from my brow. The setting sun cast long shadows, and I wonder how long I have been gone in my time. 'I must be getting back,' I say, just as I see a head bobbing up from the brambles behind the shed.

'Who's that?' I ask, pointing.

'Who's who?' Francis, who was throwing a plank of wood on the pile of rubble, comes over to look.

'I thought I saw a man in the bushes.'

Francis walks around the side of the shed to look. 'Nobody there. Are you sure?'

'I swear,' I say, but I'm so tired I can't be certain. 'I must be getting home anyway. Maybe I'll see you tomorrow?'

'There's a party at the air base on Thursday. Are you coming?' he asks.

It's the date of the Blitz, and I freeze.

Swallowing hard, I reply, 'Sure, I'll come,' and head down the grassy bank toward the lane. As I walk, I hear rustling in the hedge behind me, so I pick up the pace and sprint towards the gate.

I don't bother to open the gate, I jump over it, lose my grip, and fall on my side, hearing my mother calling for me.

'Where have you been?' she asks, looking me up and down. 'You're covered in... what are you covered in?' She rolls her eyes at me and grabs a clean towel from the pile of washing on the table. 'Boys! I don't know. Go and get yourself cleaned up.'

I look down at my clothes, full of coal dust, mud, and who knows what else. I think it's oil on my leg, but I can't be sure.

'And what the heck are you wearing?' she says, shaking her head. 'They're a size too small for you. Dan, I *have* bought you new clothes in the past year, unless you're growing faster than I thought. Come on, your food is ready.'

For the rest of the evening, we sit in the living room watching television and relaxing for the first time in ages, but my mind was far from calm. I met my great-great-grandfather today, and my brain can't quite believe it. I only wished I could share it with Mum.

'Mum, do we have a picture of Seamus?'

She looks up from the television. 'I think Gramps does. Why?'

'Oh nothing,' I shrug. 'I'm just curious to see what he looks like.'

She returns to the television show, but her thoughts seem elsewhere. A moment or two later, she gets up off the sofa like she's on a mission or something. I assume it's the picture I asked about, so I follow her through the hallway and up the stairs. 'Mum, are you alright?'

'Yes, Dan. I just remembered something. Come here.'

She walks into the spare room, the one where I keep hearing the Germans. I hesitate before stepping in, but everything seems in order.

'I thought I had a picture of Seamus,' she says tossing clothes and books out of a box. 'Ah,' she stands up straight and blows the dust off the cover of a large photo album. 'I remembered I have a picture of old Seamus at my granny's wedding.' She flips through the pages, and I feel nervous. What if I'm right? What does this mean if the man I saw in 1941 is actually Seamus?

'Here you go,' she says, turning the book over and handing it to me. She points to a faded black-and-white photograph with bent corners. 'That's him.'

I gasp. It's a picture of the family standing together outside a church, and although it's a hard shot to see, there's no doubt it's Seamus who I saw in the past.

'Are you okay?' she asks. 'Looks like you've seen a ghost?' she laughs. 'He was a lovely man. All the mystery surrounding him makes me wish I'd gotten to know him. It would've made a fascinating story for a book,' she sighs. 'I quite fancy writing another book.'

If only she knew I have that power. *Power?* That sounds like the wrong word, but now it feels right. I just don't know why, or what this power means, and why I, of all people, was able to walk back in time.

'Maybe you will...' I stop myself from saying more, even though I want to. There's no way I can tell her.

'Will what, Dan?'

'Ah, I mean writing the book, finding more information,' I shrug.

She eyes me curiously. 'Sure. I'll need to find a time-travel machine for that,' she jokes, and I can't help but think - if only she knew.

The next morning, I'm awakened by voices outside my bedroom window. I sit up and pull back the curtains to see a group of men gathered by the gate. Nothing seems odd about that, except they're dressed in khaki clothing; long green trench coats and big black boots reminiscent of the 1940s, and Alfred is leading them.

'Right, boys,' he says, as if addressing them like an officer. 'You know the protocol. Stay out of sight, and under no circumstances, give yourself away to anyone, including the lad. You're there to assist at only certain moments, moments we know will happen. Otherwise, keep your distance and observe. Time is changing constantly, especially since the lad has discovered the family.'

'WHAT?' I say out loud. I sit back down on my bed, pondering for a moment. Maybe this *does* have something to do with saving the family. Well, if this is true, I have two days to figure out a plan. I jumped out of bed, got dressed, and rush down the stairs.

'Mum, I'm off out for a bit, okay?' I call, already halfway out the back door. Just as I creep by the hedge beside my house, I see the men vanish like ghosts through the gate. I gasp, and Alfred must've heard me as he snaps his head toward me, grinning widely. He knows I was watching, but why isn't he telling me anything?

Once the coast is clear, I sidle up to the gate and walk through, rain lashing my head. I'm drenched in moments. Great! Apart from knowing the date, which is the 10th of February 1941, I have no idea what else the day will bring. I then remember the book that detailed the day-to-day events of the war and wished I'd read it for this particular day.

'Dan?' I hear a familiar voice call. It's Francis walking toward me.

'Where are you off?' I ask, wondering how he knew I'd be here right now.

'To the cottage,' he nodded to my home, except it isn't my home right now, not since I walked through the gate. I look back. 'Oh? Is everything all right? I thought you said the guy who lives there is an oddball?'

'He piques my interest, that's all. Are you coming?'

'Um... I think I'll pass,' I say because if I walk through the gate again, I'll be back home. In my time.

Francis pulls his jacket over his head and looks like he wants to say something but can't quite formulate the words. The rain beats against his face, and he blinks away the raindrops weighing down his lashes. 'Dan, can I tell you something? But if I do, please don't panic.'

I feel cold sweat forming on my brow. I think I knew where this is going. 'Course you can.'

'I've known since the day we met that you come from a different period of time. You're a time traveller!' he says, almost too casually for my liking. It's not as if you meet one every day. How does he know?

My mouth is as dry as the Sahara, and I don't know how to respond. I thought it was supposed to be a secret, and if I'm meant to save the family from the bomb...

'Yes,' I croak. 'I'm a-a time traveller.' The rain is lashing down so hard now, and my brain is muddled by his revelation. What if this affects time? Or the future?

'I knew it!' he grins and slaps me on the shoulder. 'This means Fritz's machine works.'

'His machine? And that's good news?' I ask, too stunned to say anything else.

'Yes, because it means my theory is right. Come, let's go somewhere quiet to talk.' He heads toward the cliffs, and I follow. The clouds begin to clear, revealing a blue sky.

Chapter Seven

Francis leads me down the stone steps and onto the beach. At this point, I'm tempted to get out my phone and start snapping pictures, but I remember he doesn't even know what a mobile is, and I'm not sure what I am supposed to say or do.

The tide is out, thankfully, and the rain has cleared, so we walk across the sand toward a boulder and a rock pool. Francis leans against the boulder, and I can't wait to hear what he has to say. He rummages in his pocket and takes out a paper bag. 'Want a sweet?' he asks, and I think a bit of sugar may help the shock, so I take a red, sticky, hard-boiled sweet and pop it in my mouth.

'So, what's the theory?' I ask, rolling the sweet around my mouth.

Francis sits up and tucks his legs to his chest. His face lightning up with pure joy. 'Well, you know how secretive Fritz is, and the fact that he has a German name?'

'Yeah,' I nod. 'He created the time travel machine that enabled me to come here.'

'Yeah,' Francis says, 'but that's not all. I think he's working with Hitler!'

Francis laughs as the sweet falls out of my mouth. 'Are you serious?' I say. I'd already seen the meeting in the back bedroom with the Germans, but how would he suspect?

'You see, I overheard Seamus talking to him one day when I was in the house. They were both speaking German, but occasionally Seamus would switch to English. I heard them talk about a meeting to hand something over to the Germans.'

'So that makes them guilty? They could've been talking about anything,' I say, hoping it isn't true, though I already suspected it. And Seamus? No wonder there's so much controversy over his story.

Francis shakes his head. 'Nah, Fritz had something in his hand, like a machine of some sort. He was definitely asking Seamus to help, almost pleading with him. And since then, Jack and I have been keeping an eye on the place, and then you showed up.'

'Right,' I nod, trying to take all this in. 'Why don't you tell me you knew I'd time travelled before?'

'Because I had to be sure you weren't also working for the Germans. I know you aren't now, after helping us build the shelter.'

I splutter. 'ME!? Work for the Germans?' I laugh. 'Not in a million years, but I think you might be onto something with the device. I can't explain fully now, but we need to find out where and when they intend to collect it. There must be a reason they want it.'

We agree to keep each other posted on anything unusual when we hear what sounds like people talking, but it isn't English.

"War haben zwei Tage, bis dahin mussen wir uns verstecken."

'It sounds like it's coming from the cave,' Francis whispers. 'Germans?' He jumped off the boulder and hides behind it. 'Hide, you don't want them to see us,' he says, yanking my jumper.

We crouch, peering over the edge. 'Possibly real Germans, or someone who knows how to speak German.' But as soon as I say that, I realise it's a stupid thing to say. Speaking German on British soil right now was a pretty dangerous thing to do. 'Sounds like it's about two days. That's as far as my German goes.' We can't see anyone in the cave, so we decide to leave the beach. We ran back up the beach and the steps, bumping into the Home Guard on a training exercise.

'All right, sonny?' says Mr Granger. 'Where are you two off to, then?' he asks.

Francis and I exchange a look. Telling him about the German would expose the time-travel device. I don't think it would be a smart idea right now, but then allowing Germans to be on the loose isn't either. But I don't have to make the decision, Francis does it for us.

'He can't swim,' Francis laughs, jabbing his elbow into my side. 'Isn't that right, Dan?' He gives me a look that says, just shut up about everything, and I nod in agreement.

'Yeah, scared of the water,' I say, and we both run across the field back to the farmhouse. 'Thanks for making me sound like a wuss,' I grin.

'You're welcome,' Francis laughs. 'I couldn't think of anything else to say. We need to figure all of this out before we tell anyone. The thing is, we don't know who is suspect right now. Anyone could be masquerading as a German, even Seamus or Mr Granger.'

'True,' I say. 'But Seamus? Do you really think so?'

'He speaks a bit of German, so that gives him an advantage.'

I sit down on the grassy bank by the entrance to the farmhouse. 'I have something to tell you. Seamus is my great-great-grandfather.'

It seems Francis's eyes are about to pop out of his head. 'Are you serious?' He sits down next to me. 'That really puts a different spin on things.'

I nod. 'Yep. He doesn't know me, obviously, as I've never met him before. I don't think he even knows I exist, to be honest.'

'Wow,' Francis whispers. 'Unbelievable!'

'I know, right?'

'So, what's the plan? Do you have one?'

'I think we need to find out when the Germans will come for the time-travel device and go from there. Maybe I need to talk to Seamus - I don't really know, to be honest. I'm just as confused as you as to why I'm here.'

'I could've sworn I had baked two loaves this morning,' cries Mrs Granger as we walk into the kitchen. She's standing, hands on hips, staring at the almost bare cupboard. 'I know I did, but I can't think for the life of me where I put it.'

Francis sits at the table and points at an empty chair for me to sit down. 'What's that, Mrs Granger?' Francis asks.

She turns to face us. 'Have you taken it, Francis? I won't be mad if you have.'

'No, I wouldn't steal from you. My mum would give me a right old slap if I did.'

'True enough. You do have remarkable manners, I must say. She raised you properly, can't argue with that.'

It was then she notices me. 'Oh, hello dear. I fear I may be losing my marbles.' She laughs as she begins to slice the loaf in front of her. She hands us both a slice each and puts a small amount of butter and jam next to the teapot. 'Share it, please. It's all I have until next week's rations. I don't know,' she says as she walks out into the garden, 'things seem to be missing here a lot lately.'

'What're you thinking?' asks Francis, noticing I'm staring into space.

'If things are going missing here, who do you think is stealing? Who would want food?'

Francis thought for a moment. and then it's as if a lightbulb goes off in his head. 'Germans!'

'Exactly,' I say. 'They may be even closer than we think.' And then I remember the bobbing head behind the shed.

I leave Francis as it's getting dark, worried Mum will think I've gone missing, so I head onto the path toward the gate when I hear whistling. I dive into the hedge and crouch, trying to focus in the darkness. There's no moon tonight, and it was cloudy.

'Who's there?' I hear a man ask. 'Come out, come on, I have a weapon,' he says, and I hear the click of a gun. My entire body quivers with fright, and I place my hands up in front of me. 'It's just me, Danny,' I say, for whatever good that may do. Apart from the Grangers and Francis, nobody really knows me here.

'Oh, it's you,' he says, and I realise who it is. Seamus. 'You gave me a fright, you did. What are you doing out here all on your own at this hour?'

'Heading home,' I say.

'And where might that be?'

'Um, just over there,' I point, but I doubt he can see my hand in the darkness.

'Come on, I'll walk you,' he says, and I feel a stab of panic in my chest.

'No, it's okay. I'm capable of walking in the dark, thanks. Plenty of practice.'

'You're funny,' he says. 'I've never seen you around here before. Which part of the country did you say you come from?'

'Um, London, but I'm staying with family right now.'

'Are you? Would I know them?' he asks, and I almost want to answer yes, you do, but I hear a dog barking in the distance and footsteps heading towards us.

'Everything all right, Seamus?'

It's Alfred! Even though his voice sounds different, I recognise it and the stench of cigars he smoked.

'Oh hello, Mr Thomas. I'm just making sure this kid gets back home safely. Says he lives over that way somewhere.'

I still can't see him properly, just an outline in the darkness.

'That's all right, Seamus. I'll take care of it; you get back to your post.'

'No problem, Mr Thomas. See you, kid,' he says and continues on his way.

I stand for what feels like minutes, waiting for Alfred to say something, when he takes my arm and walks me hurriedly to the gate.

'Listen, Dan, things are getting dangerous here and I think we ought to talk.' I catch his face in the glimmer of the cottage light, and he looks so much different. It's like he has had cosmetic surgery or something. His skin is youthful, his face is thinner, and his hair is darker and shorter. A lot different from the electric socket look he wore back in 2022. 'See you on the other side,' he says and pushes me through the gate before I have a chance to say anything.

Chapter Eight

The sun blazes down on me, and I turn back to where I had come from, wondering if I must have been dreaming it. Surely it can't have been Alfred. He looks younger than his years. I'm just about to head back to my cottage when Alfred steps out of the bushes. An older-looking Alfred with unruly hair and a scowl on his face. I hoped that isn't directed at me, or maybe he always looks like that; I'm not sure.

'All right, Danny boy,' he says, his eyes glinting as if he's caught his catch of the year.

'Morning, Alfred,' I reply.

'It's afternoon, kid. Come on, come to my place for a cuppa. I need to talk to you. I don't care what your Gramps says, you need to know.'

'What do I need to know?' I feign ignorance, still unsure if it was him who shoved me through the gate.

'You'll find out soon enough, come on. Time is really of the essence here, Dan.' He hurries toward the castle; his wax coat flowing behind him. I turn toward the cottage and wave at Mum, who is tending to the garden.

'Where are you off?' she asks.

'Just been invited to tea at the castle,' I say smugly. 'Maybe the queen is in residence, 'I shrug, and she laughs.

'Al; right, just don't be late.'

Alfred lifts the iron-wrought latch on the wooden door and gestures me inside. 'After you,' he says, and Jess bolts through the door before me, making me laugh.

'Wait here,' he says, and I find myself standing in a dimly lit hallway, a musty-smelling hall with a wooden floor and a knight in armour standing proudly watching me. Of course, it's empty, but I can't resist taking a peek, so I lift the helmet. Thank goodness - there isn't even a skeleton!

As Alfred's footsteps echo down the hall, I wait nervously to see what's coming.

'Come here, kid,' I hear him call, so I rush down the hall to a door that's open just a crack.

As I'm about to step inside, my mouth drops in shock. The room is full of tables, with people rushing around on headsets, dressed in 1940s military clothing. But if that's not strange enough, there's a gigantic screen propped on the wall showing footage of the farmhouse. *What* is going on?

'Dan, over here,' Alfred waves me over to a desk beside the screen. As I'm make my way through the throng of people talking away into their headsets or to each another, I realise what this must be - the epicentre of the time travel operation. They've been watching from the other side!

'What's happening?' I ask, flopping down on a chair. I can't take my eyes off the screen. Now I see Francis and Jack kicking a ball around the garden and Mrs Granger calling them for dinner.

Alfred snaps his fingers in front of my face to get my attention.

'Sorry, I-I I think I'm in shock or something...'

'You're not in shock, you silly boy. You've already travelled through time, so this is nothing. This,' he gestures around the room, 'is the hub. We've been watching you closely, Dan, for a very good reason. Now, what your grandfather doesn't want you to know is that you were chosen to undertake this task way before you were born. Let me start from the beginning, shall I?' He snaps his fingers at a man in an RAF uniform, who brings over a plate of sandwiches and a drink and sets them in front of me.

'Eat,' Alfred says. 'The queen isn't in residence by the way, but you are now part of Her Majesty's secret service, if you will.'

I stuff a ham sandwich in my mouth and mumble, 'What?'

Alfred laughs. 'Since the war ended in 1945, and since the discovery of Fritz's time travel device, which you possess, by the way, we've been watching the past, so to speak. That device is extremely dangerous in the wrong hands - German hands. We know their intention is to change the outcome of the war should they lose - which they did, thankfully, but time can still be manipulated. The past exists, and that device still needs to be closely watched, and that's what we do.'

'Right,' I say, still trying to process everything 'So, you're watching now because you're afraid it's about to end up in German possession? But, how when I have it?' I took the watch out of my pocket.

'You don't understand, Dan. The past keeps repeating itself, in many versions, in fact. We just happened to stumble upon this event just before you were born. Your grandfather and I have worked together on this project for many years. He only became involved when, one day, while watching the screen, you appeared on it. We somehow had to get you here at this moment to do what you are meant to do.'

'What am I meant to do?'

'We've only seen snippets, and we don't know whom you're meant to trust or not yet, because time is changing all the... time, basically. But we believe this is the final replay of this event. Why? Because the watch is slowly losing its power.'

'It is?' I look at the watch. 'How do you know?'

'Because Fritz is my grandfather, and I have read all his books.'

I gasp! 'For real?'

Alfred nods. 'For real.'

I look up at the screen and see Francis sitting on the back doorstep, his hand on his chin as though deep in thought. Something I already know.

'Can I trust you?' I ask Alfred.

Alfred lets out a laugh. 'I hope so,' he says, and winks.

'But I saw you back there as a young man,' I say.

'So you did. For us, we become our younger selves when we go back. I don't quite understand my grandfather's reasoning for this, or whether it's just a glitch, but that's why you're the one doing this, as we've discovered the device only works and stays at the age, you'll be in both worlds at thirteen."

'Wow,' I shake my head, staring down at the pocket watch that's ticking erratically.

THERE IS NO TIME FOR sleep. I need to get back because tomorrow is when the bomb is going to hit the farmhouse. It seems I'm meant to save the family, especially the boys, for some reason. I don't know how or what I'm going to do, and Alfred can't offer any help as nobody knows quite for sure how anything is going to play out. Whom do I trust? Well, the only ones so far are Francis and Jack.

I leave the castle more confused than ever. As I'm heading back home to let Mum know I won't be having dinner, I see Gramps leaving the gate and heading toward the house. Did he just time travel? Is that where he's been?

'What's he doing?' I whisper, hiding behind a tree so he doesn't see me. Once he's gone inside, I dash toward the back door and stumble into the kitchen.

'All right?' I ask as they sit at the kitchen table having tea. I pretend I don't know anything about Gramps travelling through the gate or what Alfred had showed me.

Gramps put his cup down. 'There you are. How's it going, Dan?'

Mum lifts her head from a book she has in front of her. 'You're out all the time lately. How are your friends? You should invite them over for tea.'

'I'm not sure if they'll be allowed.' I reach for the cupboard and take out a packet of ginger biscuits. 'Mind if I take these?' I ask, and before anyone can question me, I'm back out the door and walking through the gate again. Only this time, I'm more on alert.

As I'm walking to the farmhouse, Francis runs down the lane toward me. 'I wondered when you'd be back,' he says, eyeing the packet of biscuits in my hand. 'What are those?' he asks, and I can almost feel his hunger.

'Here,' I offer him the packet. 'You can have them,' I say.

'Cor! A whole packet?' His eyes widen. 'Must be so handy living in the future, eh? I bet you got lots of yummy things to eat.'

'You may as well have them all,' I say, making a mental note to fetch more goodies next time, even though I'm not sure I'm supposed to. I can't see what harm food would do. 'So, have any other things happened since I've been gone?' I ask as we walk toward the cliffs.

'Yes, in fact, Fritz's place has been busy. People are coming and going. I see them sometimes from my bedroom window. And Seamus has been acting oddly. He comes to the house with Mr Granger after Home Guard duty, and he's been very quiet. Not like his usual self.'

'We need to figure this out and soon,' I say.

'Yeah, we must. There may even be an award in it. Shall we go for a walk?' he asks. 'The RAF do their training today, and I love watching them.'

'Sure, why not?' I reply, and we head towards the cliffs.

'What's your favourite plane?' he asks as we walk down the path.

'Spitfires, of course. You?' I ask.

'The hurricane. She's an absolute beauty. I hope to be a pilot when I grow up. Just hope this blasted war is over first, though,' he laughs.

I don't have the heart to tell him it would be another four years yet.

'What about you?' he asks. 'What are you planning to do?'

I had to think about this. Once, I told Mum I wanted to be a writer and a historian like her and Gramps, but now I think I wanted to join the RAF too and serve my country like all the brave men and women of World War Two did.

'I think I want to be a pilot too,' I say, now imagining myself sitting in the cockpit, fending off the enemy in combat.

Chapter Nine

Sitting on the cliff's edge, munching ginger biscuits, Francis reaches into his jacket pocket and pulls out an envelope.

'I got a telegram from Mum,' he says. His head dips as if he's about to cry. 'Our house got bombed two days ago,' his voice catches in his throat. 'We've nothing left, so Mrs Granger has asked mum to come and stay. She'll be here in a few hours.'

His news shocks me, especially since he's been so calm about it - until now. I put a comforting hand on his shoulder. 'I'm really sorry, Francis. But at least your mum is safe. That's the main thing.'

'Yeah, that's what Seamus says. Things can be replaced, but not people.' He wipes his tears with the back of his hand.

'So true,' I say, thinking of my dad who walked out and left us. He hasn't been in contact since. I don't know why, but I hope it isn't because of me. There's nobody to get answers from, and even Mum is confused.

'Do you have brothers and sisters?' he asks.

'Nah, I'm the only child. Dad left a while ago and hasn't been in touch at all. So, it's just me, my mum, and Grandad.'

'My dad left too, when I was a baby. It's hard,' he sighs. 'Sometimes I wonder if he thinks of me at all, but then he might've been called up and got killed. I suppose that's why I've been interested in the time machine; you know? So, I could go back and get him.'

I nod in agreement. 'Yeah, that would be a great idea, but I'm not really sure if time should be messed with. Look what it's caused so far.'

'Or is about to cause,' he says, and I agree again. 'What's it like where you live?'

'Back home in the future? It's different,' I say, not sure where to start. 'There isn't a world war, but there's always someone fighting in some far away land over something or other. If it's not politics, it's religion. Stupid it is,' I say, spitting the words out.

'So, we won the war?'

'Yeah, we do, but because of this stupid time machine, it could all be reversed.'

'That's a worry, but it's great that we won,' he says, punching the air as a Spitfire roars across the sky. I get up and wave, and my heart swells with pride at the magnificent machine.

'Yeah, a big worry,' I say. Then something makes me pause, and I sit back down. 'Do you really think Seamus is on the side of the Germans?'

A seagull swoops down, almost snatching the biscuit from my hands, and we laugh.

'It's possible, but I've known him for a couple of months now and he's always nice to me, so I can't say for sure, to be honest,' Francis presses.

'Yeah, it's a difficult one, isn't it? But Fritz... I have to say, I did see something at my house once and it felt as though he was being made to do...' I stop, wondering if I'm revealing too much information, but what does it matter now? He knows about time travel!

'What's that?' Francis presses.

'Oh, that I think he's being forced to work with the Germans. I have reasons to believe he's innocent,' I say. 'I think it has to do with his time-travelling device.'

'I think I understand,' he says, and I nod.

'Well, then we need to stop the Germans from getting it. But how? How is it possible that they're here in hiding? Oh my God, the food keeps going missing. They've been stealing from your place!'

Francis almost spits out the biscuit he's chewing. 'The bread!'

I don't know how to explain the rest: the Blitz and the stray bomb hitting the farmhouse. Of course, I can't tell him any of that, so I wonder how I'm going to stop a group of Germans from stealing the device and save the family. I need help.

'Boys!' comes a voice from behind us. It's Jack.

'What do you want?' Francis asks.

'Dinner is ready,' he says, eyeing the biscuits. 'Wow, can I have one?'

'Here, greedy guts,' Francis laughs, and we get to our feet and walk to the farmhouse.

I'M DEEP IN THOUGHT as we walk back. Somehow, I have to make sure Francis and the family attend the party tomorrow and don't stay at home. But why wouldn't they go, anyway?

As we were near the entrance to the farmhouse, Francis points toward Fritz's cottage.

'Who's that man?' he asks. 'Never seen him sniffing around here before.'

I look at the young man with short dark hair, wearing a plain shirt and grey trousers, talking to Fritz in his garden.

'No idea,' I say.

'I saw him come through the gate, you know the one where you come from,' he says.

'Did you? But that doesn't mean he's from my time or even a time traveller,' I say, hoping the latter isn't true.

'I think so,' Francis says. 'He appeared like a ghost. One minute he wasn't there, and the next he just appeared by the gate.'

I take a look at the man again. There is something familiar about him. 'Really?' My head is now swirling with thoughts. Gramps? It could be, but why would he talk to Fritz?

'Earth to Dan?' He snaps his fingers by my face, and I jump out of my thoughts.

'Sorry, miles away,' I say.

'Seems like it. Come on, let's go and have a nose.' He smiles mischievously and sneaks across the hedge, crouching down.

Fritz is standing with his back turned to us, talking to the stranger. Now and then, I catch glimpses of the man's face as he speaks. German? But Gramps doesn't speak German, I'm sure of it. But hang on, didn't Mum say to ask Gramps about some German words not long ago? But is it Gramps? I can't recall any pictures of him when he was younger to compare.

'What's he saying?' Francis whispers.

I press a finger to my lips and shrug. They continue to speak when I catch something I recognise. 'Caves' and 'midnight.'

A clatter in the kitchen prompts Fritz to head inside, and it's then I see the full face of the man standing in front of him. It is Gramps! He can't be on the side of the enemy, can he? Is that why he hasn't been around?

I gasp, and he must've heard, as he comes to inspect the bushes. 'Anyone here?' he asks, now in English.

Francis's eyes are wide, and I mouth to him not to move a muscle.

'Ah, Herr Bauer, komm herein,' Fritz says, leading him into the kitchen before looking around and closing the door.

'What was that about?' Francis asks, getting to his feet.

I turn away and pull out my phone, quickly googling the words I heard to make sure I was right, surprised it even works here. Maybe Alfred did something to the watch to enable technology to work here? 'I think he saod something about caves and midnight. Other than that, I don't know. We'd better go, come on.'

'Well, that's obvious, isn't it? The beach. They're planning something, I know.'

I have a feeling he's right.

We're strolling toward the farmhouse when a black car pulls up. We stop and wait to see who emerges. Just then, Jack runs down the footpath, screaming happily.

'Mum, Mum...' he yells, and Francis joins in as well once he realises who it is, then runs toward the car too.

The door opens and out comes a tall woman in a green coat. She has light-brown hair in curls, and as soon as she sees the boys; she drops her suitcase and runs toward them, arms outstretched.

'Oh boys, I've missed you so much!' She pulls them in for a tight hug. 'How have you been?'

Jack jumps excitedly. Mr and Mrs Granger emerge from the house, followed by Seamus.

'Hello,' says Mrs Granger. 'So nice to meet you at last,' she says telling Mr Granger to take her bags, but before he can, Seamus steps forward.

'I'll do it,' he smiles at the lady.

Francis calls me over. 'Come and meet my mum. Mum, this is Danny, my new friend.'

She smiles and offers her hand. 'Hello, Danny, Francis mentioned you when I spoke to him on the phone the other day. So nice to meet you at last.'

'I hope the journey was pleasant?' says Seamus, shaking her hand. She looks like Vera Lynn, the singer.

'Come on, you two,' Mrs Granger says. 'I've made a tea for your mam's visit, but don't bloomin' ask where the Welsh cakes have gone. I put them in a tin when they cooled, and they've also disappeared.'

Francis and I share a look.

Sat around the table, Mrs Granger pours everyone a cup of tea. 'Sorry if it's a bit weak,' she says. 'I put this week's rations aside and I'm missing almost half. I don't know! I swear we have ghosts.' Once she's seated, we all tuck into our Welsh cakes. I spread the thinnest amount of marge on mine while Francis delves into the jam pot.

'You've arrived just in time for the party tomorrow,' Seamus says.

'Oh,' she says, and put her cup down on the saucer. 'What party is this?'

'It's put on by the air force,' Jack chimes in with a mouthful of cake.

'That sounds lovely. I'll have to see if I packed my frock.'

I notice Seamus and Josephine exchanging glances.

'I have several if you need one,' says Mrs Granger. 'Though you're a lot thinner than me, so we'll have to see,' they both laugh.

All the talk of tomorrow brought me back to the bomb. How am I meant to make sure the family stay at the party?

I check the time. 'I'd better get home,' I say. 'Thanks for the tea, Mrs Granger, and nice to meet you, Josephine.'

Seamus gets up and follows me out. 'Wait up, kid!'

Oh no, what does he want with me now?

'See you later, Dan,' Francis winks, and I nod. I guess I'm coming back later, then.

'I'll walk you to the gate as I'm headed that way,' Seamus says.

'It's fine,' I say, now panicking.

'Nah, I have something to ask you if that's all right.'

'Oh yeah?' This doesn't sound good.

We're heading toward the gate, and I'm walking as slowly as I can while I try to come up with an excuse not to go through.

'So, do you like it here, then? Better than London, I bet?' he asks, and I'm sure this isn't what he wanted to talk about.

'Much,' I say. 'At least we're not getting bombed,' I lie.

'I suppose there's that,' he laughs.

I'm trying to hold it together at this point as I'm talking to my great-great-grandad. If only Mum could be here to talk to him. I try to think of what she'd ask.

'Why can't you join up like the rest?' I ask, thinking I may have overstepped.

'I'm partially deaf in my left ear,' he says. 'Do you know I'm the youngest Home Guard they've got? It's my biggest achievement,' he says, and I think if only he knew what I knew. 'I'm doing my bit anyhow,' he shrugs.

'Of course you are. I mean, you're patrolling the cliffs for Germans,' I say. 'Keeping us safe and that.' I hope it will encourage him to talk.

'I hope I'm doing just that - keeping you safe,' he says with a hint of sadness. 'Sorry kid, I'm dumping my troubles on you,' he perks up again. 'So, what I wanted to ask was, do you think it'd be okay with Francis and Jack if I ask their mum to the dance tomorrow? They're your friends and I don't want to upset them.'

I'm relieved. 'Oh, well, I can't see it being any harm.'

'Of course.'

We reach the gate, and I halt, trying to think of what else to say. 'Um, so, if you were to encounter Germans on the cliffs, what would you do?'

He looks perplexed. 'Well, um, I would arrest them, of course.'

'Right,' I nod. Surely, he isn't a secret German. I'm sure of it. But his great-grandson? I have no clue right now. It seems that both my grandads are mixing with the Germans in some way, and it isn't good.

I have one hand on the gate, about to push it open, when I'm saved.

'Seamus?' Mr Granger calls. 'We're needed at the cliffs.'

He turns to me. 'See you later, kid.'

'Yeah,' I reply. 'See you.'

As I'm about to go through the gate, I see a face in the upstairs window of the cottage. Fritz. But it's too late to do anything about it now that I'm back home.

Chapter Ten

A hand clamps down on my shoulder. 'Danny, there you are!' It's Alfred, and he has a scowl on his face.

'What have I done now?' I ask.

'It's not what *you* have done. Come on, we can't talk here.' He grips my shirt as we walk toward the castle. 'It's about your Grandad.'

'Which one?' I ask.

'Norman. Who do you think?'

Well, apparently, I have two, but one lives in the 1940s and doesn't know me. 'What's happened to him?' I ask, trying to unhook myself from his big hands.

'That's just it. We don't know,' he whispers and shoves me through the door. He checks nobody is watching, slams the door shut behind him, and asks me to follow him. I tug down my shirt and straighten myself up, but Alfred is urging me to move faster. 'Time is of the essence,' he says, taking a turning down a hall. He unhooks a key from the chain on his trousers and opens the door that reads, 'Enter at your own risk. I will not be responsible for what the dog will do.' I think about how small Jess is and burst out laughing.

'That's enough of that, thank you,' he snorts and gestures me inside.

'My private space,' he says, pointing to a black, leather chair. 'Sit down,' he says curtly, and I think there's no need for the rudeness. I survey the room - what a mess! Stacks of yellowing papers are piled high in front of the desk, if you can call it a desk - it may not even be a desk. It could be a dinosaur knowing him. Bookshelves fill every wall space and are stuffed with leather books, files full of loose papers, dirty cups, and photo frames full of black and white pictures of people.

'What's happened?' I ask, turning my attention to the chair, which is also full of papers. I decide to stand.

He steps over a box spilling with yet more books and sits behind the desk, his hands clasped to his chin. 'I wondered where he'd been skipping off to, and now, I find he's over there talking to Fritz. What's his game?'

'What? You mean, you don't know either?'

'I wouldn't be asking you if I did, would I?'

'Well, I don't know either. I thought you two were friends and working together, but since I saw him there, I don't really know for sure who to trust.'

'As I said, Dan, this is the last time this part of the past gets replayed. And we haven't seen this version before, so we don't know. In each version there are little changes, sometimes so subtle we can't tell the difference, but since now your Grandad has been there, believe me, this is a massive change.'

'Can't I just ask him when he comes back?'

'No. You must never talk of it; it could change yet more things we can't anticipate. Like, I won't ask you anything even though I've seen most.'

'So, what do you need me to do? There's supposed to be a bomb explosion tomorrow and I need to make sure the family stays away from the farmhouse. Plus, there's something going on with Fritz and my grandads. This is hard.'

His face softens. 'I know, Dan. But this is important work. Fritz - my Grandad wasn't a bad person...'

'I know - I saw him in the back bedroom. It was sort of like a projection of the past playing out in front of my eyes. He was urging me to help him, I think.'

'I don't believe it's him we have to worry about.'

'Dan, where have you been?' Mum asks as I stroll through the back door. 'It's late and you haven't had supper - or dinner. And don't even get me started on Dad. I do not know where he's off to lately. Probably drinking with Alfred.'

I slump down on the chair. 'Probably.' *Or maybe with the Germans.*

It was then I notice Mum has several boxes around the living room floor, all opened and teeming with photos and letters.

'What's all this?' I ask, getting on the floor. Images of people in black-and-white photos stare back at me, but I don't have a clue who they are.

'Family, Dan. They're all family. I forgot Mum had given me this box before we moved here. 'I mentioned to her I wanted to know more about Seamus and the story, but all she could offer me was this,' she waves her arms about the mess she created. 'I'm no closer to knowing anything.' She shrugs and stares into space - which was the television.

I pick up a pile of fading black-and-white photos and sit back against the chair, sifting through them. 'Who is this?' I ask, holding up an image of an older lady sitting on an armchair with a younger boy on her lap.

'Oh, I forgot about her!' Mum reaches for the picture. 'That's great-granny, Josie, and she has your uncle on her lap.'

'Aunty Josie? I've never heard you mention her.'

'Haven't I? Oh, she was Seamus's wife, Josephine.'

'What? Really?' Josephine is Francis's and Jack's mother? Could it possibly be? 'Is she still alive?' I ask, thinking probably not.

'No, Dan. Not sure about her sons either... I can't remember their names now. It'll come back to me.'

This is amazing news. 'Mum, I'm just popping out for a bit; I won't be long.'

I slam the front door closed before she has a chance to protest.

In the cold night air, I walk down the path, wishing I could speak to Gramps. Now I know there's a reason for saving Jack and Francis, they were my uncles! But that doesn't explain the reason Grandad was fraternising with the enemies, or at least pretending to be German when he wasn't.

I only have a few hours until the start of the Blitz. I just wish I knew what was about to happen so I could save the family from potential disaster, because if I don't, there is a chance my Grandad wouldn't be born and my mum... which meant that I won't either. The thought strikes me so hard I sit down on the castle wall, and for the first time, I actually feel scared.

I stand at the other side of the gate and look toward the cottage. If there was one person who could help me, it was Fritz. I just have to ensure there were no Germans lurking first, or my Gramps.

I step through the gap in the hedge and see the kitchen door open. Just then, there's a clatter in the kitchen and the window flung open, spilling smoke and the hacking coughing of no other than Fritz, who pokes his head out of the window, gasping for breath.

'Are you all right?' I rush to the window, which is he now climbing out of.

'Yes, thank you,' he says and looks at me oddly. 'I know you, don't I?' he asks.

'I think you've seen me around,' I reply, more concerned about the fire in the kitchen. 'What about the fire?' I panic, pointing to the window, which is still spitting smoke.

He laughs. 'It's not a fire, it's just a stupid potion gone wrong, and that's all. Come inside,' he says, and I follow him through the door. The smoke has lessened now, and he leads me into the kitchen. 'Danny, isn't it?' he asks as he used tongs to pick up a glass cylinder and throw it into the sink.

'How do you know who I am?'

'I've seen you, of course, many, many times. We also met briefly in the back bedroom. Remember?'

'So, you did see me? But how?'

'Long story, Danny, and we don't have a lot of time. Well, not at this particular time, if you get me,' he scratches his head. Even he seems confused.

'The Germans are coming for the time travel device, aren't they?' I get straight to the point.

'Yes, but it's what they intend to do with it that causes me alarm. I need your help.'

'I think you do,' I say. 'The Germans need the device to change the course of the war, don't they?'

'They do and they're planning to collect this evening at 9:00 p.m., while everyone is at the party. They must be stopped.'

'But what about the bomb?'

'The bomb? Oh yes, the bomb. It happens at around the same time. That is fixed, unfortunately, and cannot be changed. We've tried many times.'

I hear the faint ticking of a clock and pull out the watch. The hands were slowing down - maybe this is what Alfred meant about it losing its power?

'Unfortunately, the watch has limited use. I say it has enough to get us through this evening... perhaps. Unless the Germans get a hold of it and change the outcome there and then.' He scratches his forehead again. There's a rustle in the hedge. Fritz leans on the sink to look out the window. 'That kid again. Come on, you may as well come inside. I have your friend here, Danny,' he says.

'You what?' Francis shrieks. He stumbles out of the hedge and wavers by the kitchen door.

'You can come in. It's not like you haven't been here before,' says Fritz.

Francis's face turns red. 'Um, yeah, about that...'

'Forget it. Of course, you'd be intrigued by my name, who wouldn't, but I am not your enemy.'

'Who is?' Francis asks and sees me for the first time. 'All right, Dan, he caught you too?'

I nod.

'Can we please stick to the task at hand?' says Fritz, looking irritated. 'There is a German here already, and I believe he is hiding in the caves. His name is Herr Hoffman.'

'Is that the one who came here yesterday?' I ask.

'Oh, you saw that too, huh?' he shakes his head in amusement. 'Yes, that's him.'

I gasp. *It's my grandfather!*

'Are you all right?' asks Fritz.

I nod. I don't even know if I can say anything.

'Well, we must convene here tonight at 7:00 p.m. sharp. Understood?'

'Yes,' says Francis.

Isn't the party meant to start at 7:00 p.m.? I wonder. *Oh no.*

Chapter Eleven

'Boys, it's best if you go. I never know when the German will show up, so better to be safe than sorry,' he says, ushering us out the kitchen door. He checks the side of the house and shoos us away. 'Tonight,' he whispers.

I check my watch. 'It's now 3:00 p.m. What do you suggest?' I ask Francis. Part of me wants to check the caves and confront my Grandad, but I'm worried it might damage the time device. We can't alert the Home Guard either, because I'd have a lot of explaining to do.

'I suggest we have cake,' Francis says.

'Cake? How can you think of your stomach at a time like this?' *If only he knew what was really about to happen, he wouldn't be suggesting cake!* 'I suppose I am hungry after discovering all that,' I say, and we walk the path to the farmhouse.

Seamus is sitting on the bench talking to Josephine, and from his smile, I can tell she's agreed to attend the party with him. *At least that's one thing sorted. I know I'll be born...* 'Oh my god!' I say out loud, and everyone turns to look at me.

'You alright?' asks Seamus.

'Yeah, fine thanks,' I reply, embarrassed.

Francis cuts a slice of cake and hands it to me.

'What was that about?'

'Oh, nothing... actually, how are you going to be at the party this evening if you're with me?'

'I'm not going. I've decided I'm helping you.'

'But you can't - I mean, you haven't seen your mum in ages; wouldn't you rather spend time with her?'

What? And miss all the excitement? No thanks.'

Bugger!

'Eating all my cake, are you?' Mr Granger booms as he strolls down the hallway to the kitchen. He's smiling and dressed in a crisp white shirt and grey trousers. Not his usual Home Guard get-up.

I don't know about these two, but someone else is,' Mrs Granger says.

'We'll find the culprit, don't you worry.' He kisses her on the forehead. 'Right, boys, what are you up to? Shouldn't you be getting washed for the party tonight? The air force kindly put it on to us, the least you could do is look tidy.'

'Who's patrolling tonight?' I ask. Surely, they wouldn't leave the cliffs unsupervised.

'Seamus has kindly offered to take the earlier shift than Mr Thomas, so not to worry.'

Francis notices I've gone quiet. 'What is it?' he asks.

I realise Alfred has his own agenda for being here, and somehow I feel comforted knowing he'll be around when it all finally comes together. 'Oh, nothing,' I say, hearing the ticking of a dying clock in my pocket.

'5:00 p.m.,' I mutter, staring at the watch.

'Boys,' shouts Mrs Granger from the front porch. 'Could you do me a favour and hop into the village to collect my vegetable rations?' She hands Francis a brown card. 'I must collect them today. Hop along before he closes.'

'Why is she worried about vegetables when there's a party on later?' Francis chuckles.

The village is one street with a few stone brick buildings: a grocer, a post office, the butcher, a pub on the corner, and a general shop with a box of newspapers outside. There are lots of men walking around in uniform. One, leaning against the wall outside the post office, seems familiar. He's peeling an apple and eating chunks off his knife.

'Alfred?' I whisper as I pass, and he smiles.

'Hey kids,' he says and offers us a slice. 'Local variety, rather juicy and sweet, too.'

'No thanks,' says Francis. 'Do you know each other?' he asks.

I look at Alfred, and he nods.

'Yeah, Alfred is helping with you know what.'

'Cor! Are you? Are you from the future, too?' Francis says a little too loudly.

Alfred grabs him by the shirt and pulls him around the corner where it is quiet.

'Kid, keep it down, will you? Careless talk and all that.'

'Sorry, mister,' Francis straightens his shirt.

'What are you doing, Alfred?' I whisper.

'You don't have to whisper, but I thought I need to be here. I cannot let you be here alone, not with your Grandad up to who knows what. I've taken over Granger's shift at the cliffs, so it gives me the advantage to stop that watch from getting in the wrong hands.'

A young woman carrying a basket of groceries walks by. Alfred smiles. 'Good afternoon, miss.' He nods for us to follow him across the road and down a country lane.

'Where are you going?' I ask. 'Do you think you should be here? I mean, you told me one little change…'

'Unfortunately, your grandfather has already seen to that. I doubt my little part in this will cause too severe damage.'

'Where are we going?'

'To the cliffs. I want to check out the cave in daylight. I want to see for myself if your grandad is there with the Germans.'

'Wait here,' Alfred instructs as he walks down the steps. Just then, a man emerges from the cave, peering around. Alfred runs back up and pushed us out of sight. We lie flat on the cliff surface and watched two men in plain clothing. One is Gramps, and he's speaking to the other in German. I feel sick to the stomach. I don't know Gramps as well as I thought. Disappointed doesn't even come close to how I am feeling.

'What's he saying?' Francis whispers.

As Alfred concentrates, he shushes me.

'He's telling him that there has been a change. The time for pickup has been changed to half an hour before the expected drop.'

'Why would he do that?'

'I've no idea right now. This has never happened before.'

'Everything alright?' It's Seamus.

Alfred gets to his feet. 'Just showing these lads what we do. Are you on duty now?'

'No, but the hut is empty. Are you on duty? Thought we'd swapped shifts?'

'Aye, we have, and yeah, I'm on duty for a bit, so what do you want?' he asks.

'The land girls saw you pass rather hurriedly; they say something may be wrong, so

asked me to check.'

'Well, all is fine here, you can go and get ready for the party.'

He looks over at the beach, and my heart races. 'Calm sea today,' he muses. 'Hope it doesn't stay like that,' he says, then goes on his way.

'He knows they're coming tonight for the watch,' I tell Alfred. 'He's working with Fritz.'

'We can't let him know about you, Dan, not yet anyway, even if he is on our side. Otherwise, it may cause problems with your Grandad,' Alfred nods his head towards the beach. 'Come on, let's get back.'

'There you are,' cries Mrs Granger. 'Where's the veg?'

'It's my fault,' says Alfred. 'I asked them to help move a few boxes outside the Pitbull Inn.'

'All for the war effort, I guess. Never mind, Francis, please go back. I promised I'd make a pie for Seamus and Mr Granger tonight when they're on duty.'

Francis huffs. 'Alright,' he turns to me. 'Don't do anything too exciting while I'm gone.'

'We won't,' I say, glad to have the time to talk to Alfred.

We sit on the grassy bank outside the Granger's property, my head in my hands. 'There are four hours until the bomb. How am I meant to keep the family away? They're going to the party, so what could possibly make them stay?'

'It's something we haven't been able to see, almost as if time doesn't want us to know. I don't know what happens, but you are meant to be here.'

It's then that we see a figure walking toward us. 'It's Fritz,' I say, jumping to my feet.

'Oh dear,' says Alfred. 'I haven't met him in his younger days.'

As he approaches, he says, 'I thought it was you from the window,' and he looks at me, and then at Alfred. 'Seems like we have a problem on our hands, don't we?'

'Alfred clears his throat. 'Could say that, yep.'

'It's fine, Alfred,' he says. 'You and I met on another timeline when I was testing the contraption, so no need to worry. As for you, young fellow, your Grandad being here will no doubt change things. It's best if you come to the house,' he looks at the farmhouse, 'I don't want anyone listening in.'

As we step through the door, the clocks starts ticking madly. 'Time is ticking,' Fritz says, 'literally. Sit down, please,' he gestures us toward the kitchen.

'It's nice to see you, Alfred. I'm sorry for the bother I caused in the future...'

'Don't mention it,' he says. 'It's an interesting life, for sure.'

'Well, we have two hours until they go to the party, so in between that time, something happens that brings them home, just before the bomb. I think, Dan, you need to go to the party and keep an eye out for anything unusual. Seamus is due to change shifts with Mr Granger at precisely 9:00 p.m. when the bomb is supposed to hit. We just have to take it from there, I'm afraid. And then at precisely 9:00 p.m., Seamus is due to meet the Germans by cliffs to hand it over, but he isn't really going to hand it over for obvious reasons, the watch has enough power to send you both back through the gate and then it'll close. Job done. I hope,' he says, scratching his chin.

'What do you mean, you hope?' I ask.

'Time isn't linear, Danny. It is an intricate spider-web of possibilities. We are controlling time here and sure, it can get messy, there are no guarantees.'

There's a bang on the door. Alfred gets to his feet and places a reassuring hand on my shoulder.

'I'll go,' says Fritz, who looks startled. He closes the kitchen door behind him, and I hear him unbolting the chain on the front door.

'Who could it be?' I ask.

'Who knows?' Alfred says, and we look toward the door.

'Yes, he's here.' We hear Fritz welcoming in whoever it is and closing the door with a thud. I freeze as the kitchen door opens and, to my surprise, in walks Francis, looking irate.

'I wondered if you'd be here,' he sits down. 'Never guess what?'

'What?' I say, thinking of all the things that could potentially go wrong at this moment.

'The party's been cancelled.' He folds his arms.

'What?' we reply together.

'How come, lad?' asks Alfred.

I see the dread on Fritz's face.

'Don't know. Something about top secret news that's come in, so the air force is on alert. So, Mr Granger has gone on lookout.'

I see Fritz and Alfred exchange worried glances. 'What do you know?' I ask.

'I did say time can be messy,' Fritz says. 'This happened in another timeline. They must be merging or something, I don't know.'

'We've got to do something now.' Alfred gets to his feet. 'Time is getting on and we don't have a whole lot of it right now. I can't believe what we thought was predictable isn't the case anymore.'

'Nothing is predictable where time-travel is concerned, Alfred,' says Fritz. 'Luckily, I prepared for any eventuality whilst I was back in the 1960s. Your father had a brilliant idea to create two watches. One in case of emergency. Danny, of course, has the original. Oh dear... I see where this is going. I have the other watch here for safekeeping. So, it is possible they still get it.'

'Clever, as I was wondering how they were going to get it from Dan,' says Alfred. 'His Grandad is the German you've been talking with.'

Fritz's face goes as white as a ghost. 'Are you sure about this? He's the one who oversees this operation to get it into the German's hands. Seamus has been helping me to plan a course of action without alerting the authorities because I mustn't allow this watch to be known - to anyone. You've already seen the dangers of it.'

'Is this why the Hub was set up?' I ask. 'To protect its existence?'

'Yes, indeed, on this very day, actually, around this very table.'

'Wow,' Francis says.

'Francis,' says Fritz. 'You must never tell another soul about this, do you hear?'

Francis nods enthusiastically.

'So, where is the second watch?' I ask. 'And why don't Gramps just give the Germans mine instead of sending me over there?'

Fritz takes a chain from around his neck, and dangling on the bottom, is a gold disc encrusted with red stones. 'I've kept it on me all this time, but nobody knows about it, I don't think.'

'We'd better hope not,' says Alfred.

Chapter Twelve

My stomach lurches with anxiety as I step out of Fritz's cottage and see the sky turn a dark, inky blue. It was just how the Germans like it - no moonlight – perfect for flying over and dropping bombs on unsuspecting, innocent people. Except, these people are my friends and family, and I can't let that happen.

Alfred, Francis, and I are just through the hedge and onto the farmer's field when we hear footsteps coming from the other side of the cottage.

'Go, go,' Fritz whispers, and I can just make out his anguished face in the fading light, his hands urgently waving us on.

I feel a tug on my sleeve – Alfred yanks us both behind the hedge. 'Shush,' he says, putting a finger to his lips.

The sound of boots comes closer.

'How are you?' asks a man with a German accent.

It's definitely Gramps.

'Fine, fine... so what's happening?'

'I've come to say that there's been a change of plan.'

'Oh?'

'We will collect half an hour earlier. Please ensure that your man is waiting on the bottom step by the beach. We will be waiting in our boat. Can we trust your co-operation in this matter?'

'Certainly. Well, you have so far,' Fritz's voice begins to crack.

'I hope so. So, tonight, after it has been handed over, your part in this will be terminated, as agreed.'

'Th-thank you. I am pleased to be of service to the Fuhrer.'

'He will be pleased to hear that.'

'I can't believe it,' I say over and over as we walk down the country lane towards the farmhouse. 'My Gramps is a German.' Every time I say the words out loud or even think it, I feel bile at the back of my throat. My chest feels like a million hammers are pounding at once from the shock and betrayal of it all. It's as if the man I thought I knew was hiding behind a mask all this time. The nice, generous, funny grandad is really an evil traitor to his own country. But why?

'I'm a bit shocked, too,' says Alfred. 'Why I didn't work this out before, I don't know. Come on, we've still got loads to figure out.'

'Oh?' says Francis, and I look at Alfred and he looks at me. Somehow, we both knew what each other is thinking.

'I think we should...' I start, about to suggest we tell him everything.

'I agree with you,' Alfred replies.

'What are you both talking about?' Francis asks, trying to wedge himself between us to catch what we're saying.

'Francis, there's something I need to tell you, something huge and important, but you can't lose it, all right? No running off and freaking out.'

He nods.

'Look, son, there is no easy way to say this, but a bomb is due to hit tonight near the Farmhouse...'

Francis gasps.

'I said no freaking out, all right,' says Alfred. 'Everyone must be out of that house before 9:00 p.m., do you understand?'

Francis nods again, probably too stunned to speak.

'The purpose of the bomb is to cause a distraction so that the Germans can get away by boat. If they do and if... if there's any damage, let's say, to the Farmhouse, they'll most certainly will get away with everything because none of us will be here if they do.'

'So... so you're saying...' Francis stammers.

I put a comforting hand on his shoulder, for all the good it'll do. 'Look, Francis, you're really important, and we can't allow anything to happen to you or your family. Can you help us?'

'Yes, yes I will,' he says, puffing up his shoulders. 'Let's get the Germans...oh, sorry, Danny, I forgot he's your grandad.'

'I forgot he was my grandad too for a moment, don't worry.' I huff. 'No German is going to be a friend of mine, not even Gramps.'

The kitchen door to the farmhouse is wide open, and laughter fills the air. We walk in to see Mrs Granger and Josephine sitting at the kitchen table, laughing over a cup of tea.

'Hello, you lot,' says Josephine. 'The party's been cancelled, so we're having our own.' I probably stare too long as she asks if I'm all right, yet my mind cannot grasp that this is my great-great-grandmother.

'Sorry, it's just that you look like my mum,' I say, remembering how she looked in her younger years.

'Oh, that's lovely. And what's your mum's name?' she asks.

'Katherine,' I reply, glancing at Alfred to make sure I haven't said the wrong thing.

'Oh, that's my middle name,' she says. 'So, we've got something else in common.'

'Yeah,' I nod nervously. Probably a lot more than she realises.

'You must miss her?' Mrs Granger asks.

'Sometimes,' I lie, knowing she is only a five-minute walk away.

Alfred clears his throat. 'It's a lovely evening for a walk into the village,' he says, hinting at them to leave.

'No, love, we're all set here. Shame about the party. I was looking forward to it.'

Alfred puffs out his cheeks and shakes his head as if to say, *women*! He taps his watch and mouths: *it's 6:00 p.m.*

There is an urgent tapping on the front door and the thump-thump-thump of feet pounding down the stairs. 'I'll get it,' cries Mr Granger. 'Good gracious,' we can hear him say. 'What are you doing here?'

Alfred shoots me a look of concern, and we head down the hallway to see what the problem is. The man standing in the doorway is Fritz!

'As I was saying, Mr Granger, I know you have had certain opinions of me, but I can assure you that I am on the side of the British,' he shouts, flapping his hands.

'All right, all right, keep your hair on,' Mr Granger replies, hands on hips and shaking his head.

Alfred moves Granger aside. 'I can vouch for him,' says Alfred. 'He is indeed a British citizen, and he is helping the war effort, aren't you, Fritz?'

Exasperated, and probably relieved to have someone stand up for him, Fritz nods. 'Yes, it's what I keep telling these people, but nobody listens.'

'I vouch for him too,' I add.

'And me,' says Francis.

Mr Granger looks perplexed as he scans our serious faces. 'Can someone tell me what's going on?'

Alfred nods. 'Come in, Fritz,' he says, and Mr Granger steps away from the door to let him inside. 'So, what's the problem?' Alfred asks, probably just as surprised as I am seeing him here.

Fritz places his hands in the pockets of his lab coat and dips his head. 'I need help. I've been working on something since 1938 - something which will help the war effort, but I am at a loss how to fix it so, I wondered since we're neighbours and all, I was hoping I could invite you and your family around for tea this evening?' He catches my eye, and I smile. 'I have a proposition. You're a man of engineering, yes?' He directs his words to Granger.

'That's right, I am,' he says proudly, squaring his shoulders.

'I have this machine I need looked at. Would you like to come over and look for me? It's terribly important it gets fixed tonight and, of course, I will pay you.'

'I'll be delighted too,' says Mrs Granger, now standing opposite Mr Granger. She nudges him with her elbow.

'Well, since the party is cancelled, I see no reason not to. Thank you,' Mr Granger says, like a man who had to swallow his pride and admit he was wrong.

'That'll be wonderful. I will see you all at 9:00 p.m., and your new lady visitor is most welcome too,' he nods towards Josephine.

Mrs Granger looks confused, as if to say how could he possibly know about her visitors?

I inwardly sigh a relief, but they haven't left the house yet and time is ticking. Most importantly, what was it that Fritz had been making?

'I must leave now, time is ticking,' he says and bids them goodbye.

'I'll walk you out,' says Alfred, and I follow.

Fritz takes Alfred to one side. 'Seamus is coming for the watch at eight. To make it feel real, I must give it to him. Be sure to stop them leaving with it at precisely 8:30 p.m., they've changed plans.'

'Gracious me,' Alfred sighs. 'I'll see you in a bit then,' he says, and they shake hands.

'Something isn't right,' says Alfred as we walk along the lane.

My heart begins to hammer in my chest. 'What is it?' I ask, but not really wanting to know. 'At least we know the family is going to be safe,' I say, thinking what else could there be?

'No, no, that is all well and good, I don't know why I don't think of that before. No, the problem is, you and you alone were meant to save the boys. You had to be here for some reason or other.'

'Didn't Fritz say that time is messy and that anything can happen?'

'That's what I'm worried about. It's almost as if we're walking blind here.'

That doesn't reassure me at all.

Chapter Thirteen

'Is everything alright, Alf?' A man in a green trench coat approaches us from the lane.

'Nah,' Alf replies, ordering me to stay where I am. 'I need you and a few others to hide by the lookout on the cliffs. Send some men up there immediately but be quiet because there are Germans about.'

'Will do, Alf,' he salutes.

Just as he's about to leave, Alf adds, 'You have my permission to shoot, all right. But not to kill.'

'What?' I cannot believe what I am hearing. 'My Grandads are there,' I protest.

Alfred turns to face me. 'One of your grandads is a German. Potentially. Plus, there are two real Germans there, as far as we know, helping him. It's just a precaution, Dan. For our safety, too.'

There is a tick-tock in my pocket, and I reach inside for the watch. When I take it out, I notice the hands are slowing down at an alarming rate. My stomach lurches at the thought of being stuck here forever. As much as I love World War Two history, I really don't want to live through it now. I start to miss my home comforts, the ones I always took for granted. And there's my mum. I imagine how lonely she'd be on her own and have to almost shake away the thought before it depresses me.

'Over there,' Alfred nods in the direction of the cottage. 'Seamus is on his way to collect the other watch.'

'It's a bit early, isn't it?'

'A little. They did say pick-up would be half an hour earlier. Hmmm. What is going on?' A rustle in the hedges startles us, and we crouch down. Just then, I hear a German accent and slowly creep up to see who it is – it's Gramps in a

German officer outfit! Oh my God, the badge belonged to him! This is where Mum found it.

'What's he doing?' I whisper.

'Wish I knew,' says Alfred.

Seamus shakes Fritz's hand at the door and then walks down the path at the side of the house.

'Something feels wrong,' I say, perhaps a little too loudly, as the next thing I see is a hand reaching for me, and I'm lifted off my feet and dragged through the hedge. Alfred yelps and comes after me, and we both look into the face of my Gramps, who presses a finger to his lips.

'What the hell do you think you're playing at?' Alfred spits. 'If I had known you were conversing with the enemy, I'd have chucked you off this project a long time ago.'

'Will you both shut up and follow me,' Gramp says. 'And be quiet, I don't want Seamus hearing anything. The next thing I know, the Home Guard will be here and then everything I've worked hard for will be ruined.' His eyes dart at something over my shoulder, and I slowly turn to see Seamus casually strolling along the path, whistling and flipping the watch up and down in his hands like it was some sort of toy.

'How do we know we can trust you?' Alfred asks, glaring at him.

'Maybe someone can help you with that. Dan, you're going to love this, come on, I want you to meet someone. Follow me, but be very quiet, there are Germans everywhere right now. They came in across the sea a few hours ago.'

'Then we should alert the Home Guard, maybe even the army!' I say, but it falls on deaf ears. He takes off across the field and I look at Alfred. 'Do we follow him or what?'

He hesitates for a moment. 'I think so.'

'What if he's double-crossing us?'

'Dan, he's still your grandad. Come on. I have a gun if anything happens.' He taps the side of his leg.

Now I feel safe. Not. I hate guns. It's probably the one thing I hate about war. People got killed, innocent people. The last thing I wanted to see was anyone being shot. I think it would scar me for life.

It's pitch-black now, but my eyes can make out the outline of Gramps heading across the fields belonging to the angry farmer, the one who hates us running across to Fritz's place, or should that be my home? 'Oh no, he's going to tell me off for trespassing!' I say, but sprint along the freshly planted vegetables anyway. Well, I don't have a choice. We come to a prickly hedge, and I shield my eyes with my arm from the y brambles until I stumble out opposite the farmer's house.

'Why is he going in there?' Alfred asks.

'Come,' Gramps waves at us.

Alfred reaches into his coat pocket and pulls out his gun. 'Just for precaution, that's all,' he assures me.

'Well, try not to use it, okay?'

'All right, don't fret.'

We come to the door, and the entire place is in blackness, so I fumble for the handle and slowly push it open.

'Hello?' I say, standing in the doorway. There's no answer and I feel a stab of worry in my chest. What if Gramps really is a German?

'In here, Dan. The room to your right,' Gramps replies, finally.

'Shall we?' I whisper to Alfred.

Alfred brushes past me and enters the house. 'I'll go first,' he says and creeps into the hallway like he's a ninja or something. If this wasn't a serious situation, I'd have laughed. I follow behind and we walk steadily toward the room. The door is open and there's a sliver of candlelight illuminating the room, but not enough to make out who is in there.

Alfred steps in and my breath hitches until I see Gramps' face glowing by the candlelight - but he's not alone. *Please don't be Hitler, please don't be Hitler...*

Around a large, rectangular table, I see the outline of several men all sitting, looking very serious. My eyes pan around slowly and inwardly freak when I see the angry farmer, but he's wearing a suit, and he's not the only one either. As I turn to the left of the table, I see a very familiar face and step back in shock - it can't be! Just then, Gramps stands up, walks around the table, and comes toward me with a big smile on his face.

'Danny, Alfred, let me introduce you to our prime minister, Mr Winston Churchill.'

The rotund man wearing a white shirt and a black waistcoat turns his head to me and peers at me over the rim of his round glasses. 'Very pleased to meet you,' Mr Churchill says and offers me his hand. 'I've heard much about you,

Danny,' he says in that clipped voice I've heard so many times while researching his speeches for projects. Alfred nudges me in the back, and I snap out of my shock and slowly walk around the table and shake his hand. *Oh my God, this is the Prime Minister of Great Britain.*

'Nice to meet you, sir. It's an honour. I mean... it's a privilege to meet you, Sir.' My arms are full of goosebumps at this point and there's a part of me that wants to ask for his autograph.

'No, I believe the honour is all mine. Welcome... to *Operation Under a Blitz Sky.*'

Operation Under a Blitz Sky!

'Really? I mean, really? I've never come across this before.'

'It's the most secret of secrets the cabinet has had to keep. This shall never be known,' he puffs on his infamous cigar. 'Right, let's get to work, shall we? I understand time is ticking. A ticking bomb more like,' he chortles, but then becomes serious again.

'Take a seat, both of you,' says Alfred, who sits next to me.

'I'm sorry I doubted you,' I whisper.

'No need for apologies, Dan. I had to keep it quiet.'

Sitting opposite me was the farmer, who is smirking. 'I'm Sergeant Hughes. I was keeping an eye on you and for any Germans that may cross the field to Fritz's place.'

'And I thought you were just a mean old man,' I say, and he laughs.

'I don't understand. Why have you been pretending you were a German? 'asks Alfred.

'All will be revealed,' he replies.

'The Germans are here, that much is true,' begins Gramps. 'For the last year or so, I have been working on an undercover operation in 1939, gaining the confidence of Hitler...'

I gasp.

'That's why you've been away?'

'Yes, Dan. With the permission of the government, I pretended to be a German and was on the side of Hitler to find out as much as I could about this time travel idea. I gained his respect and became the leading man on the mission. You see, Seamus was about to serve life, or possibly be executed for his involvement. If that had happened, none of this would be here. I had to stop that timeline from happening - this timeline.'

'I'm sorry,' says Alfred. 'I wish you had told me.'

'I couldn't risk anyone knowing. It's why Seamus' legacy is a rather confusing one. So many timelines have been playing out - some call him a hero and others think he's a secret German. I have to get this cleared up, and tonight. This is our only chance.'

'So, what's the plan?' I ask.

'Yes, about that. It has changed somewhat since Fritz has asked the Grangers around, but I'm not entirely convinced they stay there. The possibility of the family returning is great. I need someone on that path urgently with a jeep to distract them, but here's the nub. Seamus will hand in the watch at 8:30 p.m. He will then hand it to me, but something will happen around that moment that has not been seen already. Whatever it is, it involves you, Dan.'

'Me? But how do you know?'

'Because you've already been seen - remember the photograph? That's how I knew you were the one to stop the Germans. It all made sense a few years ago.'

'Oh yeah, the picture.'

'So, it's important that once we go out there, we're vigilant.'

'Yes, of course,' I mutter, feeling nervous for the first time.

'So then,' says Mr Churchill. 'I understand that we are dealing, not with a weapon of destruction, per se, but a contraption of science - still, it's destructive in the wrong hands. Tonight, we must protect the time travel device at all costs. I give my orders for its termination, and it must never be spoken of again.' He pounds his fist on the table. 'Let's stop the Germans from taking over our Great Britain!' he roars, and I can't help feeling a swell of pride in my heart.

As we exit the farmhouse, Grandad buttons up his coat and puts on his cap. I stare at him, and it chills me.

'It's alright, Dan, I hate this get-up too, but I can't go out there wearing the Allies uniform, can I?' he chuckles.

Something was worrying me. 'Gramps, what if something goes wrong? Will we be stuck here?'

'I can't answer that question, Dan. Not truthfully.'

Then a voice booms by the door, 'Never, never, never, never, never - in nothing, great or small, large, or petty - never give in, except to convictions of honour and good sense. Never yield to force,' says Mr Churchill, and he winks at me. 'I have faith in you all,' he taps Gramps on his shoulder. 'Except for that uniform,' he laughs and walks toward a waiting car. 'Good luck,' he waves and gets into the car and drives away quickly.

'I can't believe I've just met him,' I gush.

'I have been waiting for you to see this moment for so long,' says Gramps. 'He's a force to be reckoned with is our Churchill. If it wasn't for him, goodness knows where our country would be right now. I mean, in the future, but even that is in danger if we don't sort this out tonight.'

'Righto,' says Alfred. 'Time is getting on. In half an hour, I'll be there to change shifts with Granger. Seamus will hand the device to you... and, well, let's take it from there.'

I suck in a breath. My nerves are getting the best of me.

Chapter Fourteen

Gramps stoops down and gives me a hug. 'It'll be all right. I'll see you back home, if not before.'

Alfred taps me on the shoulder.

'Dan, it's time to give me the watch,' he says, and I retrieve it from my pocket. 'What if...'

'No, no... it's not the time for this. Be brave now, kiddo.' Reluctantly, I drop the watch into his hand, and he turns to Gramps.

'Here you go. Make sure you knock on the back door. We don't want to startle anyone in the house with that uniform,' he says.

'I'll take it,' Francis says. 'I'll take it to Fritz. It'll be safer.'

Alfred and Gramps exchange looks. 'Maybe it's a good idea,' Gramps says. 'Francis, make sure nobody sees you. I'll head back to the cliffs before the others get suspicious of me. The others should be arriving on the boat any time soon.' And then he leaves.

'Francis, will you be alright?' I ask.

'Of course, I've got the easy part. Good luck, Dan. I don't know what's about to happen next, I mean, I hope it's nothing but, ah... if you go back before we have time to say goodbye, I wonder, will you look me up in the future?'

My eyes well up with tears. 'Of course I will. I'm not sure if you'll know me back there from here,' I shrug. 'The time thing is messy.'

'Hopefully, I will,' he says, pulling me in for a hug. 'See you, future boy!' he yells as he runs towards Fritz's cottage.

'I'd better go and take over Granger's shift, all right. Do what you have to do, Dan. I have complete and utter faith in you.'

Suddenly it's quiet and I'm standing alone in complete darkness. The farmhouse is to my left, and the cottage is to my right. What could possibly go wrong?

I stuff my hands in my pocket and pace the field when I hear footsteps approaching.

'Jack, can you remember where exactly you put my toolbox when you emptied the shed?' says Mr Granger.

Oh no.

I edge around the bush and watch them head to the house; a flicker of a torch pointing toward the ground to show them the way. My heart is hammering! By now, the Blitz has started and no doubt the plane is on its way here, ready to drop the bomb. I'm about to rush to the house to distract them when Francis bumps into me.

'Dan! I can't stop them. Mr Granger needs a special tool to fix Fritz's machine or whatever it is. He sent me here to warn you. This machine must be repaired tonight - something to do with the gate, and only Mr Granger knows how. If the bomb...'

'I get you... this must be the change Fritz was talking about. Okay, so...' I was about to tell him my plan when a low drone of aircraft could be heard. I stare up into a pitch of darkness. 'They're coming.' I run into the farmhouse and yell, 'Mr Granger, Mr Granger...'

'Jack!' Francis shouts.

'Yeah, what is it?' Mr Granger says from the kitchen. He's kneeling, rummaging through the cupboard.

'You need to leave! Now. There's a plane,' I gasp for air. 'I hear a plane... I think it's the enemy.'

Mr Granger chuckles. 'I don't think so. If they're going to bomb anyone, it'll be London.'

'Mr Granger, please,' urges Francis. 'It's true.'

Mr Granger pauses what he's doing and gets to his feet. 'Wait a minute, I do hear something. But that could be one of our boys,' he says. 'It does sound incredibly close...'

'We can't take chances. I think... I think your toolbox is in the shed!' I yank his sleeve, pulling him to the back door with all the strength I can muster. 'We've got to get out NOW!'

Francis heeds my advice and scoops Jack in his arms just as the roar of an engine gets louder, almost overhead, and the house rattles and shakes. I push Mr Granger out the door, and we race to the shelter as the tip of the wing passes over and the ground moves beneath our feet. I reach the handle of the shelter, and we pile in just as the sound of a boom and the splattering of earth and bricks pelt at the shed like a downpour of rain and thunder.

'Jesus!' Mr Granger says. 'We're being invaded!'

Now he clocks on!

I pat around for the toolbox, remembering I tucked it under the shelf when we cleaned it out. 'Mr Granger, I haven't got time to explain,' I thrust the toolbox into his hand. 'You must fix whatever it is for Doctor Fritz. It's for the war effort. Please. I must go,' I say and push open the door, but it becomes wedged. I could see a lick of flames and blazing rubble.

'You can't go out there, boy. You'll get blown to smithereens.'

'You've got to help me, please...'

Together, Francis and I push the door, and it flings open into a cloud of dust and ashes floating in the air. Francis gasps at the pile of rubble the farmhouse had become, and Mr Granger let out a sob. 'My house, the mongrels.'

'Francis, make sure he gets there, you know why,' I say, but he just stares at the destruction, and he nods.

I cough and splutter my way across the garden and onto the footpath, running as fast as I can toward the cliffs, hoping I am not too late. I stumble onto the cliffs just as I see Alfred creeping behind Seamus, who heads down the steps onto the beach.

'Alf!' I whisper.

Alfred swiftly turns around.

'Dan!?' he whispers back and beckons me to hurry.

'Yea, it's me. Have they got it yet?'

'No, this is the moment, come on. I saw the explosion. Are the kids safe?'

'Yeah, and Mr Granger. He's going to fix whatever it is Fritz needs fixing.'

'I don't know this version, tell me when we get home.'

'If we do,' I mutter under my breath.

'Less of that,' Alfred scolds.

The tide is out, and I see a boat bobbing on the water. This could only mean one thing - the Germans are already here to collect the time travel device. We back against the cliff wall as we descend the steps so as not to be seen, and just as we reach the bottom, Alfred urges me to stop walking.

'Over there,' he whispers with a nod to the caves.

Out of the opening of the cave, I see Gramps, followed by another three men. Seamus walks to greet him when I see another dark figure emerging from the boat. 'Is this supposed to happen?'

'No,' says Alfred. 'There were only meant to be four, including your Grandad.'

'Give it to me,' says Gramps with his hand held out. 'Hurry, we don't have a lot of time,' he says, approaching Seamus.

There was a moment of silence. Seamus is standing, facing Gramps, and shakes his head.

'You're evil. The whole lot of you! Maybe I shouldn't give you this!'

Oh no, Seamus, what are you doing?

'This has never happened before,' Alfred says. 'Maybe the changes you've created have helped, I don't know right now.'

Anxiously, we stand watching the scene play out before us.

'Don't be stupid, boy!' says Gramps, and it is odd to hear it as Seamus is older than Gramps. The man standing next to Gramps pulls out a gun and points it toward Seamus.

'Why don't you just do as you're asked?' The man says in a thick German accent. 'And we can all go home.'

'This is serious. Come a bit closer.' Alfred creeps down the steps and reaches into his jacket pocket, pulling out a gun.

'For our safety, Dan, nothing else.' He points it toward the German with the gun.

Just then, the man from the boat steps forward. 'You've been instructed to deliver the package from Herr Fritz. Now hand it over before things turn nasty.'

Seamus begins taking slow steps backward. 'No. I ought to arrest every one of you, that's what I should be doing.'

The German from the boat points his gun at Seamus and Gramps reaches out his arm in defence, blocking the barrel of the gun.

'Nobody is going to get hurt,' he speaks in a German accent. 'The Fuhrer did not permit this. This had to be done quietly, swiftly, and efficiently,' he barks his orders at the man. 'Now put down your weapons. Both of you. I will deal with this.'

My chest suddenly tightens with anxiety. At this very moment in time, history is about to change for the better or worse. I wanted to run over to

Seamus and snatch the watch from him. What is he playing at? This wasn't how it was supposed to go.

'Seamus, please trust me. If you don't hand it over, it will look bad.' He walks toward him and holds out his hand.

'And let you change history? No! I can't allow it. I don't know what Fritz was thinking, helping the Germans.'

Seamus is about to turn and run when Gramps pulls him back by the shoulder and whispers something in his ear. I don't know what was said, but Seamus shakes his head, whether in defiance or disbelief, I don't know. Then, sure enough, whatever Gramps said, has worked, because Seamus hands him the watch. I exhale with relief that it was over, but then, the sudden thumping of feet down the steps changes all that. It's the Home Guard!

Chapter Fifteen

'Out of the way, lads.'

I was right; it's a group of Home Guard's and Alfred's army.

I don't think this is supposed to happen either, but I look at Alfred, who mutters, 'About time, boys.'

Just then, the Germans withdrew their guns, and the Home Guard halts, also raising their weapons. It is like a stand-off from a wild west movie.

Gramps raises his hands and, speaking in a German accent, says, . 'There's no need to shoot,' I can't help but think that if only he had surrendered to Mr Crompton and explained the situation, things might be different. But then, the German who just got off the boat grabs Seamus and points the gun at his head.

'Leave or I will shoot this man,' he threatens.

Just when I think things are about to get even messier, Gramps points his gun at the German.

'Who put you in charge? Hitler? I don't think so. Leave that man go immediately.'

'What are you playing at?' the German snaps at Gramps. 'You're playing with fire here. These are our enemies.'

'Trust me.'

The German seems to consider his options, then finally relents and pushes Seamus toward the Home Guard, who greets him with a congratulatory pat on the back from Mr Crompton. The others keep their weapons trained on the Germans, who look stunned. Even Gramps appears shocked.

Alfred rushes to the scene, and I follow. 'Arrest them all and put them in Hugh's cottage, will you? I'll get on to HQ and get this sorted.'

'Alf, what about the time? It's ticking, and we don't have much longer until the gate closes.'

'I'm thinking,' he whispers as we watch the disgruntled Germans being marched along the beach.

'I need him,' Alfred says, pointing at Gramps. 'The government would like a word with him,' he says.

'Sure about that?' asks Mr Crompton.

While the others are taken away, Alfred grabs Gramps by the scruff, showing he means business and marches him back to the top of the cliff.

'Have you got the watch?' he asks.

'Here,' Gramps hands it to him, and then to me.

'It's barely working,' I whisper. 'What are we going to do?'

'Let's just get to the cottage first.'

'While Mr Granger is indisposed, I'll take charge from here, lads,' Alfred says, opening the cottage door. 'I want those,' he points at the Germans, 'in that room, and him,' he looks at Grandad, 'in there. I'll question him until the military police arrive.'

We don't have much time. Fortunately, the guards do as he asks, and Alfred ushers Gramps into the room where we were talking with Churchill, then closes the door.

'I don't know what to do, Norm. We've got to get you out of here, and the clock is ticking.

I pull the watch from my pocket. The hand is flipping back and forth on the number five. 'It's not good.' I spy an open window. 'Look, we can leave through there. By the time anyone gets here, we could be back home, and this will be all sorted,' I say hopefully.

'Lock the door,' Alfred says, then helps Gramps out the window. I swing my legs over the ledge and hear Francis.

'There you are,' he pants. 'You've got to come and see. The gate... it's been damaged.'

This isn't what we want to hear.

'You've got to be joking!' says Alfred. 'That isn't supposed to happen.'

'But it has, and we need to sort it, come on. Where's Fritz?'

'He's in the cottage with Mr Granger, trying to fix something.'

We run all the way to the cottage, and as we reach the door, Alfred stops Gramps. 'The uniform. I think you'd better remove the coat and hat, at least, or you'll scare them.'

'Good thinking, Alf.' He took off his hat and coat and drapes them over his arm.

I was hoping he'd give them to me for my collection, but I don't recall Mum ever finding them in the shed. Alfred bursts through the door, and Mr Granger and Fritz look up from a semi-circular metal contraption connected to a grandfather clock.

'What's this?' I ask.

'Something wonderful, I hope,' says Fritz. 'Pass me the spanner, quickly,' he nods to a pile of tools on the floor.

Immediately, Alfred and Gramps rush to help with whatever it was they are working on, just as Seamus comes through the door.

'The army is on its way, Alf, what do you want me to do?'

'We need a cuppa tea,' says Mrs Granger, pottering around the kitchen with Francis's mum.

'Tea!' Mr Granger exclaims. 'At a time like this?'

'Keep calm and carry on,' she sings.

I pull Francis aside. 'Do they know what's going on, then?'

Francis nods. 'Yeah, since I already knew, Alf thought it was best to tell everyone. He had word from the future that it was all right to do so, so we've all been sworn to secrecy, even though it took Mrs Granger some time to recover from the shock. I think she's still in shock, to be honest.'

Mrs Granger emerges from the kitchen with a tray laden with mugs. 'I always thought there was something odd about you, Danny,' she says. 'But I'll keep your secret for you, no worries.'

'Thank you,' was all I could muster.

Seamus is halfway up the stairs. 'I'll keep an eye out,' he says, raising his binoculars.

'We will, too,' Francis and Jack squeal, running up the stairs after him.

I turn to Fritz. 'What are you doing?' I ask. 'Is that thing a time-travelling machine?'

'Yes. A time portal, like your watch, but bigger.'

'Is this because the gate outside is destroyed?'

'Yes, I had this idea before the watch version. It was partly made before the Germans arrived back in 1938. Once it is activated, it will send you home.'

'The watch won't work otherwise?'

'No, not to go back to where you came from,' his face softening. 'Don't worry, it will work.'

I manage a weak smile. 'I think I'll go and help Seamus,' I say, thinking about Mum.

In the back bedroom, Seamus, Francis, and Jack are huddled by the window, binoculars pressed to their eyes.

What if I get stuck here? I begin to wonder. What would Mum do without me now that Dad is gone? Tears prick my eyes as a low rumble from downstairs shakes the bedroom floor.

'Danny? Are you up here?'

I gasp and turn toward the bedroom door. Seamus, Francis, and Jack do the same.

'You hear my mum?' I say, barely believing it.

'What's happening?' Francis cries. 'Something feels really different here, do you feel like time is out of place?'

Seamus puts his finger to his lips and stands. The doorknob turns, and I back toward the others. A moment later, the door opens fully, revealing my mother standing in the frame, her expression bemused and her face pale with fright.

'Mum.' I run towards her, taking her by the arm. I can't believe I can touch her. I imagine we look like ghosts to her. 'It's fine,' I assure her, though I'm not confident. I have no idea what just happened, but somehow Mum is here in 1941. Or have we gone back to 2022?

'Danny, who are these people?'

'Mum, this is Seamus. Your grandfather, Seamus.'

'Not possible, Dan. I'm going to ask again; who are these people, and what are they doing in my house?' Her voice trembles.

'I can't...'

'It's fine, Danny's mum. My name is indeed Seamus, and I believe we are related.' He holds out his hand. 'There is no need to be frightened.'

Mum stares at his hand and walks slowly toward him.

'Are you... ghosts?' Her hand trembles as she reaches Seamus's.

'I don't believe so, no,' he says with a gentle smile, carefully shaking her hand.

Mum pulls her hand back. 'Oh my god, you're real,' she shrieks, covering her mouth. 'Danny, how is this happening?' Her face turns even paler.

'Mum, I'll explain, I promise, but it'll have to be later in case we don't have enough time. Remember, you wanted to ask Seamus questions? Now's your chance. Go on.'

'I...I...' She pats her pockets. 'I need a pen or something...'

I look around the room.

'Here,' Seamus says, digging into his jacket pocket and handing her a pencil. 'Thank you.'

'And here's some paper,' Francis adds, swiping an exercise book from a box.

'Um,' flustered, she flips open the book and drops the pencil, which rolls across the floor to Jack.

Jack picks it up and passes it to Mum.

'It's Jack and Francis, Mum. Josephine's boys.'

'Oh my god, really? I can't believe it.'

'Hurry,' Seamus urges. 'Time waits for nobody.'

'Seamus, why is your story so secret that it can't be shared with the world?'

'It can be shared. It's simple, actually. We must always stand up to bullies, whether it is a tyrant hell-bent on taking over the world through any means possible, or a kid snatching someone's lunch money. When all this is over, tomorrow morning things will be a bit different, and you'll be able to share my story with the world.'

'I can? I have your permission?'

'Yes, you do. I don't trust anyone else to tell it. It was lovely to meet you, Katherine.'

'You're fading a bit. What's happening? Dan, you too, oh my god, what's going on here tonight?' she shrieks.

Like a fading photograph, the room reverts to how it was in 1941, and Mum slowly disappears as though she were a ghost. But of course, I knew she wasn't because she hadn't been born yet, and neither had I.

There are feet thudding up the stairs. and the door bursts open.

'My god, you're still here,' Alfred breathes deeply. 'We've another means home, Dan. Fritz has created another portal, but we must hurry.'

I turn to Seamus and Francis and Jack. 'I can take it from here, Danny,' Seamus says, his eyes twinkling. 'I won't let anything destroy your future - your secret is safe with me and the lads,' he says. nodding to Francis and Jack. They both nod in turn.

'Cross my heart,' says Jack. 'I won't tell another living soul.'

'But they want Grandad - they think he's a German spy!'

'I have an idea,' Seamus says, brushing past Alfred and bolting down the stairs.

'Come on,' Alfred says to us, and we chase after him.

The pounding on the door is getting persistent, so much so I think they'll break it down.

'Can't Churchill get them off our backs?' Alfred asks Grandad.

'I've no way to contact him now. He's probably on his way back to London.'

'Great, 'Alf mutters. 'You could've mentioned this friendship beforehand. It would've saved a whole lot of bother.' he says, more to himself, and I don't think Gramps hears.

'Norman,' says Seamus, 'swap clothes, come on, we don't have a lot of time.'

I realise what he's about to do, and I know it will be the reason that everyone thinks he's on the side of the Germans.

'You can't,' I say, but he doesn't pay any attention.

'Are you sure about this?' Gramps asks, handing him his coat and hat.

Seamus nods and hands him his shirt. 'Very. I'll explain why I was undercover. It'll be all right, trust me.'

'And I will vouch for him,' says Fritz.

'It's the only way,' Alf says, looking Gramps in the eye. 'If you get caught and we don't make it back, every timeline, everything we have accomplished thus far, will have been for nothing.'

Mr Granger walks to the door. 'Are you ready?' he asks, his hand on the doorknob.

'Wait!' Fritz throws a cover over the contraption. 'Ready.'

'Wait!' Gramps grabs Seamus's arm. 'You must take this.' He reaches into his back pocket and produces a small black leather-bound book. 'This was Hitler's. I stole it. It has times and dates, plans and maps - you name it. This may be your freedom card. Churchill will be informed and will help you, too. He'll know that we've swapped places. I don't know what else to say but thank you.'

'Don't mention it. We're family.'

'Now, once you've gone,' says Fritz, 'I will also destroy everything, all of my work. No one will ever know anything about what has gone on here today,' he says, tears welling in his eyes.

I now understood why I couldn't find Seamus or Fritz on the internet. It all starts to make sense to me.

'Before you go,' says Mrs Granger. 'I want to say thank you. Thank you for bringing us hope in our darkest hours. No one will ever know except us how the war was won. I hope that one day in the future we'll see each other again, even if it's only a mere recognition, a flicker of a memory locked far away in the deepest part of ourselves.'

'I hope I will see you all again, too.' Francis puts an arm around Jack, both of them crying. 'Thank you for being my friend,' I say.

'I think we're more than that - we're family,' Francis says, hugging me, and Alfred says it's time to go.

As Mr Granger turns the door handle, we hurriedly walk through the vortex and tumble onto the hallway floor.

'Who is there?' asks Mum, wearily.

I run into the kitchen, and see her sitting at the table, her head in her hands, and used tissues scattered all over.

She leaps from the chair. 'Dan, oh thank God. I don't know if I was dreaming or not, but when I went upstairs, I saw you and you saw me because we spoke, but it felt as though I was seeing you from a different time. I can't explain it.'

'I can.'

As I'm about to speak, Grandad and Alfred, now as I recognise him in the present, enter the kitchen. Mum can see by the looks on their stony faces that something has happened.

'Is everything alright?' she asks.

'I'll pop the kettle on,' Alfred says. 'We're going to need it.'

Chapter Sixteen

Mum leans back in her chair, shaking her head in disbelief. 'I can't believe it, I really can't. But in some ways, it sort of makes sense too. I've often felt that time is out of place in this house.'

'Did you?' I ask. 'I wondered why you mentioned time travel a few times.'

Mum gasps. 'I did? Oh yeah, I did too! How strange is that? I never thought about why.'

'Don't overthink it,' Alf laughs. 'Trust me, time is a very confusing, somewhat complex thing. It's has given me headaches more than once.'

'And me,' Grandad says, stirring his tea. 'Not to mention Hitler. What a crazy man!' He shakes his head solemnly.

'You'll have to tell me more, Dad,' says mum. 'I could write another book.'

I roll my eyes. She would write a book about anything. 'The problem with that, Mum, is who would believe it?'

'Oh yes, I hadn't thought of that.'

Alfred sighs. 'No matter what we did to change the outcome of the war, the history books will always remain the same. We were merely ghosts passing through a time that has already happened. Our efforts were subtle, nothing to shake the foundations of the era, but enough for those in the know,' he adds with a wink.

'We need a day out, Dan,' Mum says, packing a picnic basket. 'We've got a lot to talk about and to digest, haven't we?' She closes the basket lid and grabs her coat from the chair.

I agree. 'Gramps, are you coming?'

'Why not? He folds his paper and sets it aside. 'It's not like I have to traipse around wartime Germany anymore, is it?'

We leave the house on a cool, sunny day. Golden leaves shroud the path to the front gate.

Alf waves from the castle, which plans to re-open to the public now that all the time travel equipment is gone.

We reach the gate. 'I miss going back to the past,' I say. 'Even though there was a war on, life seemed better without all the technology. People talked. Families sat around the table at mealtimes...'

'I know, Dan, I really do. We need to make an effort to have more family time.'

Grandad pauses by the gate, one hand on the bolt. Mum sucks in a deep breath after learning what has happened. 'It'll be fine now, won't it?' she asks nervously.

Grandad snaps out of his thoughts. 'Yes, it's closed. I doubt we'll ever be able to go back again,' he says, pushing the gate open.

As we walk through, I expect something to happen, but it doesn't. It is 2022 and the path to the farmhouse is as normal as ever. As we walk further along, a car is parked by the entrance to the farmhouse.

'I wonder whose car that is,' Mum says, as nosy as ever.

Grandad wanders over to take a look. 'Come here,' he says, waving us over.

Walking around the ruin are three men. One is stooped with a walking stick, and the other two are middle-aged, pointing at the remains of the building and chatting excitedly.

'Are you alright?' Mum calls out. 'I believe this is private property.'

The elderly gentleman turns around and waves.

'Do they know us?' I ask.

'Don't know,' Grandad replies. 'Only one way to find out, isn't there?'

He marches ahead and waves back. 'Are you lost or something?' he asks.

'Not quite,' the elderly man replies. He's wearing an RAF jacket with a bar of medals across the left breast pocket.

'Would you be uh, Norman?' he asks, then looks at me. 'Danny, isn't it?'

'How do you...?' Then it dawns on me, but it can't be... 'Francis?'

Mum gasps. 'Francis Jones?' Mum says. 'Are you really? Oh, my lord, you're Seamus's stepson, aren't you?'

'I am indeed, and these are my sons, Jack and Matthew.'

'I can't believe it,' I say. 'And you remember me, too.'

'Well, of course, I remember you, Danny. You saved my life. I expect it's only been hours for you, not years,' he says. 'And I may have gained a few more wrinkles, but I'm still me.'

'What are you doing here?' I ask.

'Oh, after the Grangers, bless their hearts, passed away, they left us the land. We own it now, but we're thinking of rebuilding it exactly as it was.'

'You own this - oh my,' Mum beams. I know what she's going to ask next.

'I wondered if you would care to join us for a picnic,' Mum says. 'We're practically family.'

Francis smiles; his green eyes twinkling in the sunlight. 'That would be splendid. Oh, before I forget,' he reaches into his jacket and hands me a newspaper. 'This is the least I could do. Seamus was a good man and the best dad I could ever ask for.'

I unfold the newspaper and to my surprise, on the front page is a picture of Seamus in his Home Guard uniform with the heading:

Local WW2 Hero Honoured for Bravery Against the Germans

We sit on the cliffs when we hear the low drone of an aircraft.

'Is that a Spitfire?' I jump to my feet.

'I believe it is,' Grandad says. 'Isn't there an air show on?'

Just then, out of the clouds, in a perfect V formation, three Spitfires and a Hurricane fly over and dip their wings towards us in a salute. I feel a swell of pride rising in my chest and salute back.

'Just as good as the old days, isn't it, Dan?' says Francis, standing next to me, munching on a ginger biscuit.

I smile. 'Yeah, just like the old days.'

Even though the old days weren't so long ago, not to me, anyhow, they'll always be in my heart, just like the people.

Epilogue

Five Years Later

THE FRONT DOOR OF THE cottage is open as Danny pulls up in a taxi, and the front gate swings on its hinges as though someone had been in a rush to leave. He thanks the taxi driver, grabs his kitbag from the back seat, and pushes open the gate, calling for his mum.

'Anybody home?' he yells down the hallway, but it's quiet as a church. It isn't unusual to leave the door open here, as apart from tourists, the place was safe. But something feels wrong in his gut. He leaves his kitbag in the hall, steps outside, and goes around the back. It is then he hears a commotion over at the farmhouse.

Since Danny has been training with the RAF, Francis and his sons have rebuilt the farmhouse to its original glory, but Francis' health has been waning of late and so he had rushed back home to see him.

Standing by the gate that five years previously took him to WW2, his arms feel prickly with goosebumps. As he unbolts the latch, his breath hitches with the anticipation of what could happen, but when he pushes open the gate, it is still the present day. Secretly, he hoped to experience the sensation and thrill of time travel again, but it wasn't meant to be. The time portal was closed. Alfred had assured him it would never re-open after destroying the watch and all of Fritz's research. He said that it wouldn't be safe in anybody's hands as the temptation would always be there, whether for good or evil. Danny agreed but was disappointed he would never see any of his friends again as they were in 1941.

As he walks down the path, his phone buzzes with a message.

'Come to the farmhouse, quickly.' It was from mum. The urgency of the message has him running to the entrance of the farm and as he ducks his head around the corner, an ambulance passes him, already taking Francis away.

'Am I late?' he asks breathlessly to his mum standing on the porch.

'By ten minutes. I'm so sorry.'

Crushed by the pain of having lost one of his best friends, mum puts her arm around him and guides him into the farmhouse. 'I've called Matthew and Jack. They're on the way.'

Today is also the first time he had been in the new farmhouse and as he walks into the kitchen, he sees Francis and Jack and Mr and Mrs Granger around the table as though it were yesterday. But it was only a memory of long ago.

'He left you something on his dresser. Let me get it,' she says and takes off upstairs.

Danny fills the kettle and sits down at the wooden table. The last time he had been in the kitchen was in 1941, when he tried to save Mr Granger's life from the Germans. He could almost picture Mr Granger under the kitchen sink looking for his tools. A moment later, the back door opens, and for a brief second, he expected a younger Francis or Jack to wander in covered with dirt after dodging Farmer Hughes across his field, but to his surprise, it was Alfred and his grandad Norman.

'Dan, I thought it was you,' says Alfred, still wearing his long green coat and big black boots. Jess strolls in behind Norman, barking excitedly when she sees Danny. 'I was finishing a tour of the castle when I saw you get out of the taxi… what's going on?' Alfred's face falls when he realises. 'Oh no, he's gone, hasn't he?'

'Yeah, not long ago.'

'Your mother says that he wasn't feeling too well last night,' says Gramps. 'I tried to get here as fast I could…' he says, waving his mobile phone.

Gramps hears the kettle boil and gets some mugs from the cupboard. Just then, they hear mum's feet thumping down the stairs.

'What's got you in a hurry?' asks Gramps.

'I'm glad you're here,' she says, a hint of panic in her voice. 'I just went upstairs and swear I hear people talking like back at our place…'

'It was us,' Alfred laughs.

But mum's face remained stoic and pale. 'No, the voices of kids... even the atmosphere felt different, like I walked into someplace else...'

Alfred and Gramps exchange looks.

'What do you mean?' Danny asks, getting up from the chair.

'You've got to come up and see for yourself, but first, I found this. He wrote this for you, Dan.' She hands him an envelope.

'Open it,' Gramps encourages him.

Danny tears the envelope and pulls out a yellow sheet of paper and unfolds it. In cursive writing, he reads aloud:

Dear Danny,

By the time you read this, I will have passed over, no doubt, onto that next great adventure in the sky. I don't wish you to be upset over my untimely death because it isn't real. Time isn't real either. I overheard Fritz explain to Seamus one day whilst nosing in his house that time isn't linear, and we could access many timelines if we knew how.

This letter, however, was written in 1945 at the exact moment the war in Europe ended, but I slipped back only a few hours ago to do so. How did I do it? Well, come and see me again at the Pitbull Inn in the village. Alfred doesn't know this, but Fritz left me with a replica of your pocket watch before he passed away. He said there was one more job to do, and we were the ones to do it. I will see you in an hour's time.

Regards,

Francis.

ABOUT THE AUTHOR

Kelly Hambly lives in Swansea, South Wales with her two children. She is a professional editor by day and an author by night. If you enjoyed Under A Blitz Sky, you may also like Nell's War, a WW2 historical fiction set in Swansea.